A GENERAL THEORY OF TEARS

KEITH RONDINELLI

A GENERAL THEORY OF TEARS

STALKING HORSE PRESS
SANTA FE, NEW MEXICO

CONTENTS

The life of man entire is misery:
he finds no resting place, no haven from calamity.
But something other dearer still than life
the darkness hides and mist encompasses;
we are proved luckless lovers of this thing
that glitters in the underworld: no man
can tell us of the stuff of it, expounding
what is, and what is not: we know nothing of it.
Idly we drift, on idle stories carried.

—EURIPEDES, Hippolytus

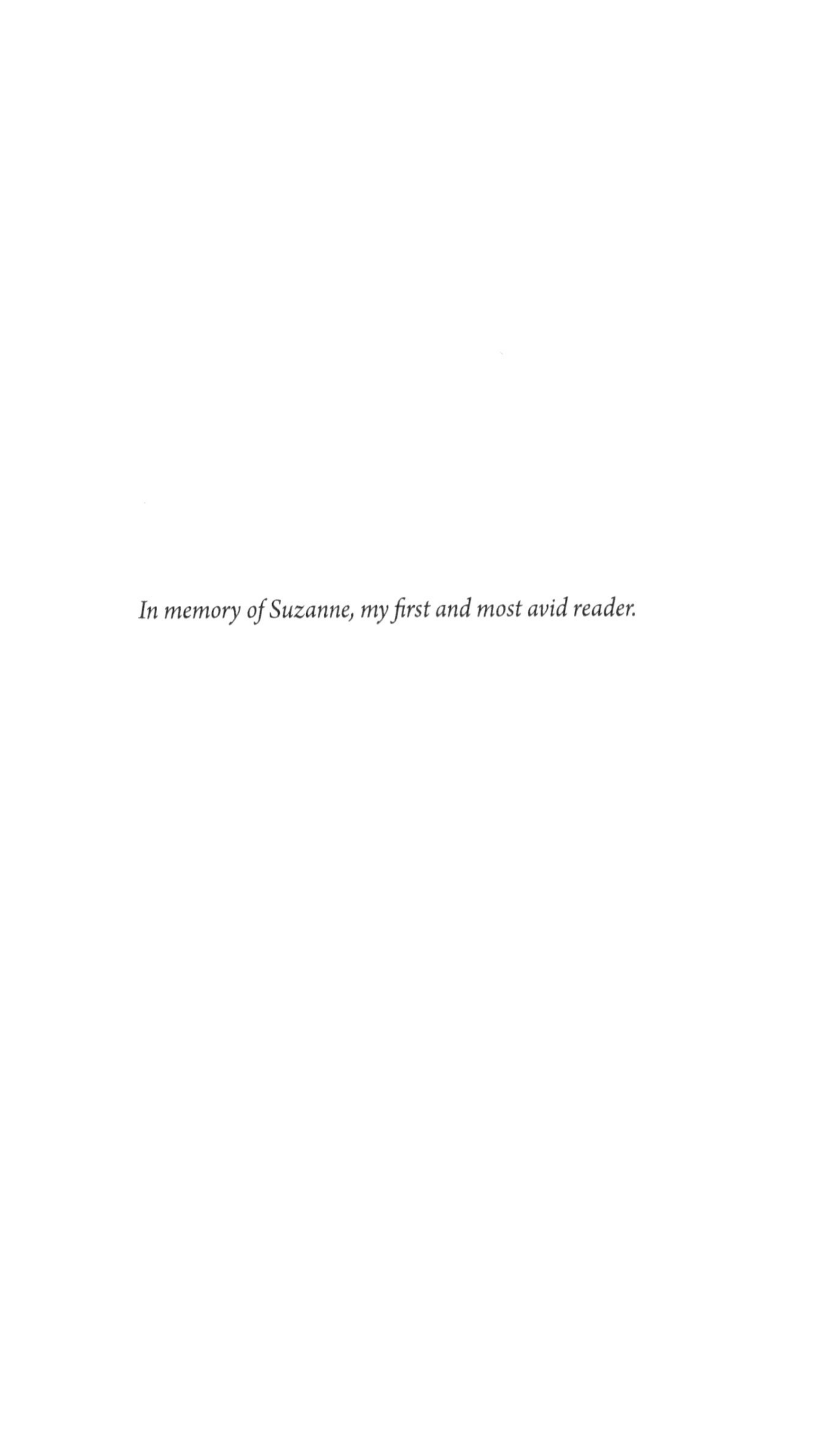

In memory of Suzanne, my first and most avid reader.

HORN

i. Flood

THE FLOOD is in the corner of the yard, beyond the swing set. Lily stands looking at it in the ragged evening light. Through the window I watch her shake her head. It is clear I am to blame.

She calls me out under the moon to consult. I express disbelief that something as arrogant as nature could have created this hazard. The crickets sing a lament. Over the fence, the dead glow of a neighbor's living room window produces a feeling I can't place. In the pallid light, Lily resembles a particularly healthy cadaver. She kicks at the ground and says, "Harris will track mud in the house. The ferns are drowning. Something must be done."

In the morning, I call a specialist recommended to me via an online community message board. His name is Trevor, and he arrives in a blood-red pickup. He wears a bandana and shin guards. He fondles a silver amulet around his neck and says,

"All the geo-engineering they're doing has been causing these strange weather patterns. Also, this entire neighborhood is built on top of a swamp. It was never meant to be."

I nod while he eyes a vapor trail's scar across the sky's skin. After splashing around in the flood, he recommends tearing up the grass and installing a drainage pipe that will empty into an underground basin lined with stones.

"When can you start?" I ask.

"When the omens are good," he answers.

ii. Neighborhood

IN THE evening, I ride my bicycle through the streets of our town. The rectilinear arrangement of the houses is soothing. I admire the planning that goes into a neighborhood such as ours. It speaks of man's propensity for order and his wish to establish a truce with nature.

The houses are lined up like circuits on a board. The sidewalks exist in a harmonious relationship with the streets, the lawns, the patios. We have designed these things to fit together, to vibrate with a resonance. If measured, I am certain the golden ratio would reveal itself in the widths of driveways, the heights of fenceposts. This convergence of angles is a bulwark against all we cannot control.

As I ride, I catch snatches of dark backyards—lawn chairs, sheds, hoses like snakes in the grass. It is scenery absent of people that most attracts me. I fantasize about walking into those lonely places and going to sleep. The odor of damp wood, wet concrete, humid lawns would be like a sleeping pill.

My nightly ride is a journey both outside of myself and

within. By disappearing into the suburban evening, among a conspiracy of sprinklers, I plot an escape into thoughts unencumbered by the messiness of other human beings. I love the world as I have created it.

I also love Lily, but she has detached herself and now floats through an opaque ether of unknown composition. Something happened to us. Much like the slowness of geologic time makes tectonic shifts ungraspable by human perception, the years have occluded the origin of our disintegration.

When I think I have arrived at the source of our estrangement, I pull back to see that this is just a small chink at the edge of a larger fissure, which is itself part of a chasm that runs down the decades to within minutes of our first meeting. Over our first drink together, our dissolution was already underway.

Sometimes I think all the love in the world couldn't save us. There is something else at work, something I'll never understand.

iii. Horn

TREVOR STARTS work on the second Tuesday of the month. He digs for a time and then calls me outside. A dog howls. Children are playing two yards over, a hectic game involving what sounds like the hammering of a metal rod on a tin can. As they frolic, they emit the shrill screams of the damned.

"I found something," Trevor says. Lily steps out onto the grass, drying her bony hands with a dishrag. As Trevor kneels and points into the pit he has dug, I notice a small detonation in Lily's eyes, a soaring recognition like a satellite's return from orbit.

"What is it?" she asks, her jaw like a piston. Her eyes search mine, then turn to the black hollow in the ground. The sinew in her neck is an aileron. All of her pieces fit together, but taken individually remain mysteries, parts to which I've lost the assembly manual. In the face of this confusion, and despite the wall between us, she is my strength. If I ever fell apart, I'd be unable to put myself back together.

"It was buried under a shelf of clay," Trevor explains. He climbs down into the hole and offers up the object to us. I glance at Lily, who doesn't look at me. I take the thing in my hands and brush the loam from its ridges. It is a piece of stone, about seven inches long, carved in the shape of a bull's horn. It has deep notches cut into one of its sides; in the reverse are inscribed several occult symbols reminiscent of hieroglyphs.

"I don't like it," Trevor says, packing up his equipment. "I have to get going, I'll be back Monday to finish up."

I give the horn to Lily and she turns it over in her hands. "I'll take it inside," she says. I picture her inserting it into her body, a missing piece much like myself, wishing to be returned to its wholeness.

iv. System

I DRIVE to work with the sun in my eyes. I think of Lily, and of our son Harris. Two weeks ago, Harris started kindergarten, and our house has suddenly gone silent. It has been difficult watching our child pass through the necessary stages of separation from his mother. As he makes his way in the world, I am reminded that I, too, am taking my first steps away from her.

I work northeast of town, in an office building along the river, for a firm called Applied Coherence Systems, Inc. The work is steady, unvarying, and challenging up to a point. At parental get-togethers, when asked what I do, I am loath to answer. If pressed, I say, "I write firmware-level code for metrology devices which measure, down to the micron, the topology of machine-tooled surfaces for aviation industrial applications."

ACS, Inc.'s building is a box composed of beige cinderblock walls and amber-tinted windows nestled among a patch of white pine and oak. There are no other buildings nearby. The asphyxiated trees provide little shadow. I take my lunch on the bank of the indifferent river. I watch the seasons turn and then retreat to my cubicle where nothing ever changes. The consistency of the office environment suits me well. I depend upon it for support as a fuselage relies on its struts.

At work, I'll often become aware of the river—its endless flow, the bits of detritus caught in its current, the wildlife beating out their unceasing rhythms. I have a recurring daydream in which I stand on the river's bank, raise my hand, and the water stops, frozen in time. Minnows are caught in mid-jump; birds in mid-flight. Exalted, I reshape the landscape with my hands, as a potter turns a pot. I return from this dream feeling indestructible. I most often have this fantasy during team meetings, when my own thoughts are subsumed into the hierarchy. Like rain on an ash pit, the life of business smothers my internal spark. Some men might see this as an affront, but I am grateful—there is such a thing as too much yearning.

On my drive home, I wind along the river. There is a grand comfort in driving, being suspended between two places. At work, I am often eager to leave; at home, I dream of returning to work. All my life I've felt there is no place for me except inside my head. Yet my mind rejects my body and plagues me with thoughts of death. The only escape is to the underworld of sleep, but the illogic of dreams is another a blind alley. I yearn to disappear into Lily, but her doors are closing, her lights turning off one by one.

v. Closet

Lily places the horn on the top shelf of our closet. We each have our own side. I've neatly arranged mine, yet classifications are loose. It is not uncommon to find a T-shirt in cohabitation with a polo. Lily's side, however, is pristine; each item is sorted based on her immutable sartorial taxonomy. Mismatched items must never touch. This taboo is one of the fundamental laws of our bedroom.

She tosses the horn onto the top shelf. This lack of concern for proper placement is uncharacteristic of her.

I ask her what she plans to do with it.

"It's none of your business," she replies.

In his room, Harris is playing Humpty Dumpty. The story of the poor egg has wormed its way into our son's subconscious to a degree I find alarming. We have sought out every book available. We have hunted down Humpty toys, clothes, silverware. Other children in Harris's peer group have had their imaginations co-opted by the latest mega-budget family entertainments. Because of this, and despite my concerns, we have invited Humpty to take his place in our family as a permanent presence. He is now one of us.

I suspect Harris's fascination with the nursery rhyme has to do with how organized his life is under Lily's tutelage. His days are planned down to the minute. His meals are scheduled in advance, as are play dates with friends, trips to the bathroom, and extracurricular activities. Even spontaneous play is plotted within the trajectory of a day's rigorous chronology.

I lament this controlled environment in which our son is raised, but what is the alternative? When we were children, our days were like bags of marbles spilled across the floor. What did all that freedom buy us but a deliberate dive into an overdetermined life? Perhaps Harris will use what we have built for him as a jumping-off point into a less structured existence, as a skydiver leaps into the fathomless blue.

In the kitchen, I fix myself something to eat. Our refrigerator resembles that of a forensics lab, each item locked away in its own color-coded container, each dovetailed perfectly with its neighbors into a cubiform puzzle almost theoretical in its exactitude. The same butter knife must not be used in two different condiment jars, lest contamination occur. Fingerprints on stainless steel are a catalyst for lectures on the careful use of faucets and towels. In our house, there is a place for everything. Sometimes, I wonder if there is a place for us.

vi. Cart

LILY HAS tasked me with procuring items from the local big box. The cavernous extremity of the store sends my head spinning. The smell of roast chicken follows me through towering aisles of haircare products. I cannot locate the particular conditioner Lily requires. Confusion leaches into my perspiration, which evaporates under a cooling vent. My melancholy is now a part of the store's vast fabricated weather system. I picture clouds of other shoppers' sorrow billowing through the fluorescent sky like thunderheads.

I throw items in a red cart with a spastic wheel. Mute children glare at me from forests of clothes racks. I muscle my way toward the checkout aisles. I look at the items in my cart and wonder how they got there. This train of thought extends to the store itself: how is it stocked? Do shipping trucks arrive under cover of darkness? I envision highways, warehouses, cargo containers, monstrous aquatic vessels scraping clandestine arcs across the globe. This elaborate system makes my products appear as if by sorcery. There is such beauty in this that I feel lucky to be alive.

When the cashier inquires, "Paper or plastic?" I opt for plastic. Plastic is more masculine. The modern ecological lifestyle is symptomatic of a larger anxiety, one that is mythic in structure and embedded within a strand of time that flows back to primordial eons. Time is a spiral, one which winds ever-upward. At any given point, we find ourselves overlapping a previous epoch, startled by the realization that our anxiety is age-old, immutable, and always linked to death. To choose paper is to admit death's power; to choose plastic is to laugh in its face.

In the parking lot, a lone empty cart leans among a patch of gray weeds. I wonder how it got there. I watch the cart recede in my rearview mirror until it is the size of a piece of candy.

On my nightly bicycle ride, I return to the lot whose giant sodium vapor lamps illuminate the empty blacktop like docking spaceships. The cart is still there, its plastic skin a bruised purple in the half-light. I sit, soaking in its utilitarian design. Divorced from the terrible beauty of the store, I can appreciate it as a thing apart from itself. Do others view me this way? Am I more than a husband, a father, an employee?

I snap a photo of the cart on my device for future reference. With this image I hope to have captured something of its soul, and by proxy, mine.

vii. Bed

I TURN over in bed and feel a sharp pain. Lily, with her back toward me, says, "Be careful." I peel back the sheets to reveal the horn. In the dark it resembles a talon. Through the window, a crescent moon provides enough light for me to appreciate the horn in its hidden glory. It is a thing that has inserted itself into our lives, and, lacking any function, asks us to provide it one. I call up the photo of the shopping cart. I wonder if the cart will be dug up by a future civilization who will try to attach totemic significance to it. What will it mean to them? Will it be the embodiment of a deity? A demon? A spirit guide?

I realize that Lily and I have only spoken of it as "the horn," yet perhaps it isn't a horn at all. Perhaps it is something else—a tool, an ornament, a device by which to measure time. If the seven notches represent days, there are only two days left in its portentous calendar.

I watch Lily reach out blindly for it, pull it close, and nestle her cheek against the horn's sensual curve.

In the morning, I descend the stairs to find Harris playing with the thing. He is running from room to room, horn held aloft, making explosive noises with his mouth. He thrusts it at me like a dagger and says, "You're dead."

THE HORN sits between us on the dinner table. It has a place setting. I ask Lily why, and she insists we must welcome it into our family.

"But it's not a person," I say.

"Neither is Humpty Dumpty," she says, pointing at Harris's Humpty doll, seated next to his high chair.

"Yes he is," I say.

"He's an imaginary egg," she says.

"But he's an anthropomorphized egg."

"He's a metaphor."

"For what?" I ask.

"Your precarious position."

"Fine, he's a metaphor. But the horn is just a thing. My position is precarious?"

"The horn is so much more than a thing," she says. "Last night, I held it against my beating heart. An entire world opened beneath my feet."

I reach for the horn, but she gets to it first. "Give it to me," I say.

"Why don't you ever touch me?" Lily demands, brandishing the horn like a frontier gambler wields a pistol. There are tears in her eyes. They are gelid, like ice.

"Why don't you ever touch me?" I ask.

"Just like a man. Answering a question with a question."

"Give it," I say, grasping for the horn.

"I have to go change," she says, getting up and taking the

horn with her. I picture Lily bringing it into a secret place and reciting incantations, whereupon her body mutates into something no longer recognizable as human.

As she leaves the room, I receive the impression that she whispers something to the horn, and then bends her ear towards its flared end as if listening for an answer. Instead of walking upstairs to our bedroom, she descends to the basement. I wait and wait some more. I give up. Upstairs, I crawl into our forbidding bed alone, where sleep takes me out of myself.

ix. Dream

TWO DAYS pass, an eternity during which Lily does not return from below. We communicate via muffled thumps and shouts. I gather she needs time alone with the horn. I wrestle with a feeling of impotence. I take Harris to school, where I am scolded by other mothers for improperly following the lot's rigid drop-off rules.

When I pick Harris up, he asks, "Did Mom come up yet?"

"No," I say.

"Have you visited her?" he asks.

"No. Have you?"

"Only in a dream."

"What happened in this dream?"

"Mom was the size of an ant. She was in a garbage dump. A gigantic robot came and carried her away. I tried to save her, but I couldn't."

"That sounds scary."

"Not as scary as real life," the boy says, staring through the

window. We drive in silence for several minutes. And then
Harris says, "Dad?"

"Yeah?"

"When do you think Mom will come up?"

"When she's ready."

That night, I tuck Harris in with his Humpty Dumpty doll.
I notice one of Humpty's seams has burst. A hernia of cotton
stuffing protrudes from the wound.

"What happened to Humpty?" I ask.

"He's coming apart."

"Well, we'll have to fix him."

"Don't you know? You can't put him back together."

x. Fingernail

IN THE morning, I awake to rain. The house is in tatters. Lily's
side of the closet vomits clothes. There are muddy footprints
across the carpet. Wet leaves stick to the stairs like decals.

"Where's Mom?" I ask Harris. His clothes are mismatched,
his hair is lopsided. There is a crust of a sandwich on the
floor, and the windows are flung open. A spray of rain has
swollen a stack of magazines. A savage wind pushes a puddle
across the hardwood. Candles are burning, and someone has
painted indecipherable words on the wall. Among the twisted
letterforms I recognize the symbols from the horn.

"I don't know," Harris shrugs.

"What does that say?" I ask, pointing at the graffiti.

"How should I know?" he says, aiming the horn at me and
winking, as if sighting down the barrel of a gun.

"Why aren't you at school?"

"Mom said I don't have to go."

"Today, or ever?"

"Ever."

"Of course you have to—"

Just then, the front door opens and Lily stomps in. She is wearing a miniskirt and stiletto heels and heavy makeup. There are terrifying rips in her pantyhose. Her cheeks are ruddy and webbed with veins, like those of a revived corpse. Her lips are swollen—she's been kissed, and not by me. She spins her car keys around on her index finger, her sharp crimson fingernail tracing unstable loops. There is such arrogance in this gesture that I feel my heart leap like a startled toad.

"What's happening?" I ask.

"Something beautiful," she says.

"Something terrible," I say.

"Something crazy," Harris says, and then yells, "Pow!"

Lily whispers: "Something you can never understand."

A CLEAN SLATE

i.

I MOVED to White Willows after accepting a position at a nearby information technology firm named CleanSlate Solutions. The development was a pristine place, scrubbed of history. Like a thousand other master-planned communities throughout the Midwest, its bucolic name belied an essential inauthenticity. They had fabricated the Willows with scientific accuracy to appear wholesome, tumbling, serene. As a writer of computer code, I found this fascinating. It was an elegant simulation.

Because I was single and childless, I was free. I came from the city with the attitude of a frontiersman. Perhaps I could forge a life here. I brought nothing with me except a wish to be welcomed.

On the first day, I took a walk under the pale noonday sun. Sprinklers chattered. Swing sets gathered rays. Moms in synthetic pants pushed strollers down freshly paved streets. With my swarthy complexion, I received a few strange looks, although I will admit this feeling could have been born from my insecurity.

I passed by a polished SUV and caught myself in its reflection. I am of Italian ancestry, but have repeatedly been mistaken for Middle Eastern. I'm certain, if analyzed, other nationalities would rear their faces in my DNA.

Once, on a cheerless city street, a man accosted me, demanding, "Where are you from? Pakistan? Afghanistan?"

I told him I was American.

As evening fell, I sat in the living room remembering the incident; I returned to it often. Ever since, I've entertained fantasies of invisibility. Could this be the cure for my self-consciousness? Or would this cloak only conceal my physical body, leaving my mind to wander much like it always has, in perpetual self-analysis?

I brushed the thought away and stood by the window. Up and down the street, all the homes' first floors were dark. But every other house's second-story glowed as if a community-wide ritual were taking place. I drifted off to sleep on the sofa in front of reruns. When I woke at 3 a.m. the house's second-floor lights were still burning.

ii.

It was difficult to determine the nature of CleanSlate's products and services. My assignment was very specific—the upgrading of several of the organization's disk-based databases to faster in-memory versions—but to what end the data were being used remained unclear. From the language on the firm's website, I gathered that government contracts made up much of its business, so it was understandable that CleanSlate kept its public-facing product descriptions hazy.

I spent my first day shaking hands, familiarizing myself with the network, and moving into my cubicle. The faces I greeted were cordial, businesslike, but their predominant whiteness set me ill at ease. I was determined, however, to keep an open mind. I reminded myself again that I've always been a self-conscious person. Just because I felt people were looking at me wasn't proof that they were. I was here to do a job.

I noticed that many of the cubicles were unpopulated. But there was evidence of human activity in each one: half-filled coffee mugs, boxes of Kleenex, Post-it notes. Had I arrived after a wave of layoffs? I had looked into the firm's reputation before accepting my position and all signs pointed to the fact that CleanSlate was growing faster than shareholders could have hoped.

Sandwiched between two abandoned cubes, I buried myself in work. Although in-memory databases are exponentially quicker than their disk-based predecessors, they are far more volatile. Power loss, especially during storm season, was of significant concern to CleanSlate's leadership. Memorandums I received spoke of contingencies involving natural disasters, popular uprisings, dirty bombs.

The company had tasked me with devising alternative solutions for long-term durability and disaster preparedness. I devoted the first week to researching the various pros and cons of checkpoint imaging, transaction logging, and replication. My universe was the glow of the screen. This had always been my salvation: a job well done, alone, with only pixels to guide me.

I spent long hours in the office, arriving home late at night. As the world revolved toward winter, dusk fell earlier, but the lights in my subdivision's second-floor windows burned like a constellation of eager suns.

iii.

One Saturday afternoon, I received a knock on my door. Standing at the threshold were several bright white faces framed with blond hair: a woman, a man, two small children.

"I'm Steve," the man said, thrusting out a hand.

I noticed a large fraternity ring, like a marble eye set in gold.

"We wanted to welcome you to the neighborhood," the woman announced. Her name was Tabitha. Fair, plain but pretty, cornfed. This type of woman had always been attractive to me; they symbolized a world I didn't have access to, one of picnics and beach clubs and New England vacations. As her eyes caught mine, my stomach sank.

I composed myself and said, "Thank you."

For a few minutes, this handsome family stood in my foyer and studied the framed photographs on the wall. "Your kids?" Steve asked, standing much too close to me. He was tow-headed and muscular, but sagging in the middle, like a quarterback past his prime. His own offspring huddled by his side, shyly curious. Even more so than their parents, the children were intensely fair, with platinum hair and skin like rice paper.

"No, the realtor put those here. I haven't had time to take them down," I explained. I had barely paid the photos any attention. I looked at them now. The children pictured in them were fresh-faced, gleaming, all-American.

"They didn't look like yours," Steve said, laughing. He stared at me with eyes like frozen ponds.

"Can we interest you in a welcome dinner at our house?" Tabitha asked, all teeth.

"That sounds great," I replied. Truthfully, the thought of a dinner made me nervous. It would force me to provide information about myself, things I either wasn't willing to divulge or answers to questions for which I had nothing to offer. But my desire to fit in prevailed.

iv.

AT NIGHT I went for quiet walks, turning over the work's technical hurdles. Technology, the focus of so much attention, was merely a tool. The very best software disappeared, leaving only its purpose on display. If you were aware of the technology when using it, it had failed its most important test. As I walked, I devised a strategy for not just giving CleanSlate what they needed, but something beyond: a transparent elegance that would make my work disappear as if by magic.

A noise from a backyard yanked me from my thoughts. I looked, but saw only darkness. In-ground lighting threw spindly shadows across expensive lawns. Marble fountains burbled. The second-floor lights burned, curtains drawn. Although the only one on the street, I couldn't shake the sensation that I wasn't alone.

v.

THE TIME for my dinner at Steve and Tabitha's arrived. I put on my only good shirt. My heart beat above the bed of crickets. The street's second-story lights continued to blaze, including those at my hosts' house. When I knocked on the door, bottle of wine in hand, Steve answered. He seemed out of breath, wearing a T-shirt and jeans.

"Do I know you?"

"I'm Robert, we met the other day? You and your wife invited me to dinner."

"Forgive me, I've been overworked. It was dark in your house… I thought you were… I mean, you look different in this light."

"Which light is that?"

"Please, come in."

As I stepped into the large marble foyer, I saw him glance at the ceiling. I noticed that there was no stairway where I expected one to be. This left the house with an unfinished feeling, as if it were a movie set constructed with budget constraints in mind.

"Tabitha's out with the children," Steve said. "We completely forgot. Perhaps we should order some takeout and share that bottle of wine?"

"I can come back another time," I said.

"I insist. Do you like football?"

"I don't really know anything about it."

"You must not be from around here."

Just then I heard a thump from the ceiling. I glanced up, and when I looked back at Steve, his eyes were searching mine. Then he glanced into the corner of the room, where a strange apparatus sat propped against the wall. It resembled a high-tech cattle prod, with a few copper wires protruding from its end, and a battery pack near its handle. Draped over its rubberized grip appeared to be a pair of computerized goggles.

"That's a prototype we're working on. I probably shouldn't

have left it out," Steve said, gathering the apparatus and shoving it into a closet. "Italian food okay with you?" he asked, pulling his mobile phone from his pocket.

"Reminds me of home," I said.

"Why's that?"

"I'm Italian. Mostly."

"You don't look it."

"I get that a lot. My mother is Sicilian. There might be some Native American kicking around somewhere in there."

"Well, hold down the fort, chief," he said, with a forced chuckle, and left the room. I listened to him order food while I scanned the house. A marble bust sat atop an oak table. A library of leather-bound volumes lined one of the walls. A cat curled on a snow-colored sofa. I could hear the chatter of a football game.

"I hope you're hungry," Steve said, returning. He seemed to have been on the phone too long to have merely ordered food.

We retired to the living room where we ate from styrofoam containers. Steve uncorked a bottle of expensive Bordeaux, ignoring the cheap bottle I'd brought. As he poured the wine, he prodded me for information about myself, most of which concerned my family history. He was particularly interested in when, exactly, they "came over on the boat." Throughout, he often glanced at his phone, and several times excused himself. Eventually, I steered the conversation toward more mundane matters: the neighborhood, ClearSlate's reputation as a community leader, the company's advances in analytics and data mining. Steve was a VP at ClearSlate, though I hadn't seen him around the office.

"I oversee the top-floor lab where the proprietary hardware

designs are produced," Steve told me. "It's demanding, but we can only hope we're doing God's work."

I smiled down at my wineglass. It was then that I noticed a crucifix on the wall above his head. He glanced at the end table, where a large leather-bound Bible sat.

"Are you a believer, Robert?"

"No. I mean, I was raised Catholic. But I'm an atheist."

"I see," Steve said. We sipped our wine. By that point, he had guzzled several generous glasses, and his speech was beginning to slur.

"May I use the restroom?" I asked.

"Upstairs—sorry, down the hall to the right," he said.

He turned his attention to the football game as I left him. I poked my head into the various rooms in search of stairs to the second floor, but couldn't find one. I opened and closed the bathroom door loudly, and then quickly circumnavigated the rest of the house. I backtracked and peeked in on Steve, who appeared to be dozing.

In the kitchen, I found a large walk-in pantry. I poked through many gourmet dry goods. At the pantry's rear, I discovered a small concealed door. The dovetails of the wood paneling masked its seams. I pried it open to discover a dim, narrow set of stairs leading up. Just then I heard Steve clear his throat. I backtracked to the bathroom where I flushed, ran the faucet, and hurried back to the living room.

"Everything okay?" Steve asked.

"Just a bit of an upset stomach," I said. This was not entirely untrue—the Italian food was typical Midwestern rubbish: too much cheese, too much garlic, too little substance. "I think I should get going. I have a long day tomorrow."

Steve said, "You'll feel better in no time."

vi.

THE NEXT morning, I received a memo instructing me to report to one of the large conference rooms for Team Education. As I sat down toward the back of the room, I noticed that the other attendees were dark-skinned like myself. Where had they been this whole time? And why were they all here?

The man who ran the training identified himself as Sean. He was thin, fit, with teeth that shone like pearls in the fluorescent light. He asked us to refer to him as the Leader. He explained that CleanSlate considered individualism anathema to its corporate culture. If we were to succeed, we were to disappear into the "corpus" of the team.

"Ask yourselves, am I here to advance my visibility, or am I here to be part of something larger? Am I seeking personal glory, or am I attempting to weave myself into the fabric of success?"

The fabric of success. Sean seemed proud of this metaphor, which I found nonsensical. Still, he had made his point. At the end of the meeting, the attendees shuffled out of the room. Sean paid no attention as we left.

vii.

THE FOLLOWING morning, I woke earlier than usual. The sky glowed vermilion, a portent of rain. At the kitchen window, I watched a CleanSlate shuttle bus hiss to a stop, kneel, and open its door. There was no driver. I wasn't aware that the firm had a stake in driverless vehicles. The door remained open for several long minutes, but no one got on and no one got off. The door swung closed; the shuttle groaned and sped off toward campus.

viii.

AT WORK, the data I was siphoning into my software was difficult to parse. It was highly segmented to the point of granularity. Some sections were encrypted with proprietary algorithms. But after several weeks of manipulating tables, patterns emerged. Demographics appeared to be a primary component, along with detailed genetic information and family lineages. Large swaths of the country's population had been broken down and rearranged into groupings that seemed related to eventual relocation. Medical records, psychiatric histories, and vectors of disease also were being collated. I was ignorant of privacy laws, but some data struck me as invasive, possibly illegal. Given CleanSlate's government contracts, I was certain some high-level wrangling made it appear lawful, even if the ethics were questionable.

I requested a meeting with my supervisor, Ken. I sat across from his desk and raised concerns over the data. As we talked, Ken twirled a shimmering golf club in his hand. I could see myself reflected in its bulbous head.

"What you're seeing is just a minor part of a larger picture, Rob."

"Robert. That's obvious, but—"

"We have asked you to upgrade the databases. What they contain is proprietary, and shouldn't concern you, should it? I'd like a progress report by noon on Friday. Management is getting ready for a big presentation to the higher-ups. Leadership is nervous. CleanSlate is bidding on a very large contract. The success of the bid lies partly on your shoulders."

I poked around a few of the building's floors which, while not officially off-limits, had been left out of my tour. The topmost open-access level held a slew of executive offices. As I walked the halls, white chiseled faces stared at me through half-drawn blinds. People tapped at keyboards. I noticed several more of the cattle prod-type objects I'd seen in Steve's house. The floor above housed the hardware labs, and this was most likely where Steve's office was located.

I looked up at the ceiling and tried to imagine what type of work went on up there. Most of what I'd been privy to was software, but Steve had mentioned hardware products, which remained mysterious. I thought of the object he'd shoved into the closet and a feeling of helplessness came over me.

I rode the elevator to the basement where dim banks of fluorescents led me deep underground. At the far end of a hallway, under a tentacled mass of heating ducts, I watched a man wearing a set of Steve's high-tech goggles poke the air in front of him with one of the cattle prods. When he noticed me, he turned and slipped the glasses off and on, as if testing them on me.

I thumbed the elevator's button and rode it back to my floor. In the morning, I had a voice message from Steve asking me to see him in his office.

ix.

"I'VE BEEN told you were giving yourself a tour," Steve said. His office was spartan and tastefully furnished. A framed photo of Edward Bernays hung on the wall behind him.

"I was never officially shown around," I explained.

"What is it you'd like to get out of your time here, Rob?"

"Robert. What do you mean?"

"Beyond compensation, what are you looking to gain? Where do you want to go?"

"Up, I guess?"

Steve looked up at the ceiling, and I followed his eyes.

"We focus less on ladder climbing than other companies, Rob. Here, it's about teamwork."

"I know. I was at the training."

"We've got plans for you."

"You do?"

"Would you like to come to our house tonight for a rescheduled dinner? Tabitha felt sorry that she missed you."

I thought of Tabitha, her minty eyes, her lithe legs.

"Sounds good."

"I'll see you this evening."

x.

STEVE WORE a white-collared shirt, Tabitha a pearlescent gown that drew the room's candlelight in like a prism. Light classical music played over concealed speakers. I turned over the conversation Steve and I had in his office. I came away from it feeling I was being groomed. Could it be that I would receive a promotion this early on? I was confident in the work I'd been doing, but I didn't think leadership had had adequate time to gauge its quality.

"Steve says you're I-talian," Tabitha said, handing me a glass of wine. There was an erotic twinkle in her eye.

"I am."

"I knew you were… ethnic," she said, rocking her boney index finger up and down near my chest. I pictured myself in a cage at a zoo, tourists snapping photos, eating cotton candy.

Just then, the children tore through the room, growling like wolves.

"They've been cooped up all day," Steve said. His nose was a blood-red beacon at the center of his ashen face. Soft waves of bourbon rolled off of him.

"Shall we eat?" Tabitha asked.

At the table, I picked through my chicken, which was undercooked and slimy. The wine was giving me a headache. A thump on the ceiling drew all of our eyes upward. The chandelier trembled. Its crystals twirled, twinkling. The children were beside me now, their golden bowls of hair like twin suns in my orbit.

"Robert has started his team education," Steve announced.

"That's wonderful news," Tabitha sang.

"There's been a lot of talk in the tech world with individuality and personal expression. We feel that line of thinking has run its course. The tide is turning. CleanSlate sees itself as an industry leader in a revolutionary type of corporate culture."

"I thought it sounded okay. Although I work best alone," I said, feeling queasy.

"It is possible to be alone and still integrate into the fabric," Steve explained. Something in the wine had gone to my head. I was having trouble focusing. Again, there was a thump from the ceiling. The family pretended not to notice it.

"I have to use the restroom," I said. My arms were numb. The walls spun, with Tabitha as their axis. I saw Steve and the children walking away into the darkened living room. The television flickered. I heard the whine of missiles, the chatter of machine-guns, and detonating shells. I listened to a news anchor say, "US warships have docked themselves off of the coast and are drawing heavy fire."

In the bathroom, I peed and flushed. In a wicker basket beside the toilet sat a stack of Guns & Ammo magazines. A bowl of potpourri gave off a sickly autumnal scent. I looked at myself in the mirror and saw a hairy beast staring back.

The door opened, and Tabitha appeared. She slinked into the room and rubbed up against me. "What are you doing?" I whispered.

"Come with me," she said, taking my hand. Those three words were the barbs at the end of a fishhook. They drew me through the murk of the hallway, Tabitha's stringy gown reeling me forward. She lured me into the pantry. I felt her arms close around me. Her fingernails were like talons. Her stiff lips touched mine. An erection lifted in my pants.

"You're watching history, kiddos," I heard Steve say from in front of the television. "We've been waiting for this for over two thousand years."

Tabitha opened the small door and pulled me in. My legs were mush, my lips numb from her kiss. She drew me through the house's dark musty bowels, down narrow spaces between walls, and, finally, up the hidden stairs to the second floor.

xi.

As MY eyes adjusted to the light, I found myself in a cramped, spartan bedroom. A cot with a wool blanket sat in the corner.

A rickety bookshelf stood under a window, stocked with tech manuals. A terminal glowed on a desk, its screensaver a slideshow of picaresque American landscapes—national parks, waterfalls, beaches. Opposite the computer, against the wall, was an apparatus that resembled a walk-through metal detector.

"Mahmoud, you can come out now," Tabitha said. From an umbrella stand near the door, she withdrew one of the cattle prod instruments. I watched a human-shaped hole form in the center of the room. The objects behind it rippled like a desert mirage. This disturbance grew more opaque until it coalesced into the shape of a man, dark-skinned, eyes pearly against leathered flesh. My feet gave out, and I stumbled. Two firm hands inserted themselves under my armpits. I felt Steve's boozy breath on my neck.

"Can we watch, Daddy?" I heard one of the children say.

"Get downstairs," Steve hissed.

I tried to speak, but nothing came out. My tongue lolled in my throat. Steve drew me to the bed and sat me down. Tabitha retreated to the corner. Mahmoud reached out for me, but then let his arm drop.

"Deportation. Sterilization. Immigration raids," Steve said. "These things are so barbaric. The autocratic governments of the twentieth century didn't have the technology we have today, Rob. The world has moved on! Cognitive workers like yourself are the lifeblood of the new economy. We need you. Do you understand?"

I felt a brief flare of hope. Perhaps none of this was as it seemed.

"We need you. But we don't want to see you."

"No, we don't," Tabitha said from the corner.

One of the children yelled from below, "Daddy! Can we watch?"

"Shut your mouths," Steve shouted. "Rob, what we are creating at CleanSlate is something our European ancestors only dreamt of. But we need people like you to help build it, do you see? Your job will proceed as-is. You'll continue to be compensated. All we ask, in return, is that we not have to look at you."

"I understand," I said, frightened at my words.

"You see, there is no escaping death. All the monumental works of art and literature are bulwarks against this knowledge. Culture is a grand mitigator of this anxiety. And the white European culture is the most majestic example of this. We won't surrender our heritage this easily. But you—people like you—are a nuisance. Forget all the grandiose talk about blood and soil. We just don't want to see you."

"It's simple, isn't it Mahmoud?" Tabitha asked, and he nodded in compliance. I looked at him and he returned a limp smile. I noticed Mahmoud's clothes were too big on him, threadbare, and several seasons out of fashion, as if he were wearing the hand-me-downs of a wealthier and better-fed person.

"It's time," Steve announced, lifting me up off the bed. He led me to the metal detector-like object. On his smartphone, he tapped a button that brought the instrument to life. It hummed with a celestial tone. Tabitha's fingers curled around my other arm. Her nails dug into my skin. The last thing I remember is that it felt good to be hurt by her.

They dragged me like a doll across the floorboards. As I passed through the portal, I was bathed in a divine light. A sexual warmth spread through my insides. It reminded me of summer vacations I never had, a life of leisure I never experienced. A bouquet bloomed in my nostrils: cinnamon, wheat, saltwater. I felt the weight of my bones lift. I emerged from the other side as a feathery, blank void. Steve held a mirror up, and I saw only the white wall behind me, bright as morning.

xii.

I RIDE the bus with those like me: the vanished, the hidden, the disappeared. It is fine that we do not have to look at each other. What good does looking do, when all it does is remind you of what you've lost? It is a blessing to not be seen.

To become imperceptible to other people, I have learned, is also to be invisible to oneself, and, in turn, to all of life's worries. I drift through my day as I did before, quietly and with an efficiency that strains toward grace. At night I am alone, and in this way, my newfound life isn't any different from my time before, when there was no one to see me and nobody to hold my hand. Whether through technological means or through loneliness, I realize now that this is what I have always wanted: to be free of the scrutiny of others. Still my heart beats.

DEMON

i. Clarity

SHE WOKE to fingerprints on the mirror. Before could wipe the sleep from her eyes, she was rubbing at the prints with her nightgown's hem. As they faded, she caught sight of her reflection: creases, bags, gray hairs. In the bathroom's serrated light, she brushed her teeth, exactly three minutes on the left, then three on the right, timed using her smartphone's timer.

She roused the children and went downstairs. There was a film of dust on the foyer table, rippling in the heating vent's current like a gray ocean tide. A tightness clenched her ribs, a corset that cut her breath in two. She used a damp cloth, making sure not to drive the dust into the air, where it would be free to roam and resettle. The constriction in her chest loosened. Then she remembered she'd seen dust in the corners of the living room the night before. She thought of how dust was composed of the feces of dust mites and trace amounts of meteorite particles. The stricture returned, and along with it the genesis of a migraine.

She swallowed two baby aspirin with filtered water and stared through the kitchen window. She began to feel better, but then water spots invaded her view. She pulled her spray bottle of diluted vinegar from the cupboard—commercial cleaners were toxic, everyone knew—and pumped a fine mist across the pane, wiping with a micro-fiber cloth until the window vanished into total clarity.

Total clarity. A quest for jeweled cleanliness. These were her ideals. She considered vacuuming, but would save it for later in the day. She opened the dishwasher and inspected the glasses. Stubborn hazy spots, which she'd been trying to remove for days, remained. She turned to the refrigerator and noticed water stains streaking its face like the dried tracks of tears. She sprayed a small fountain of foaming cleanser across the blemishes and wiped until the surface shone like a lake in summer.

ii. Lists

SHE CONSULTED her lists—grocery list, to-do list, school checklist, summer camp options, house repairs, birthdays, holidays. The to-do list had grown especially long:

PRINT CALENDAR FOR SUMMER CAMP

FOLD LAUNDRY

REMOVE STAINS FROM PAJAMAS

BUY PIPE CLEANERS

PAINT AND ORGANIZE PANTRY

SORT THROUGH OLD CLOTHES

BUY BIRTHDAY GIFTS FOR TWINS

INVESTIGATE DEMON IN BASEMENT

DROP RECYCLING OFF AT DROP-OFF CENTER

BRING EXTRA CHINA TO GOODWILL

Investigate demon in basement. She didn't recall writing it. As she puzzled over the words, the odor suddenly returned: sweet, putrid, alien. She descended to the basement and followed the scent's trail to a corner of the laundry room, below a corroded nest of pipes. There, in the cobwebbed shadows, she could make out a small two-by-three orifice in the plaster. The hole resembled a miniature arched doorway. She inhaled. The odor wafted from the opening, damp and putrescent.

Upstairs she added CALL HANDYMAN to the to-do list and checked and rechecked her grocery list, the kids' after-school activity list, the list she used to keep track of other lists. She moved to the living room, where the children had strewn injection-molded toys like a multicolored minefield. She returned everything to its rightful place, which produced immense satisfaction.

She opened the blinds to the sodden sky. In the yard, just beyond the windowsill, a dead bird lay decomposing in the grass. Evidence of its impact with the window—a percussive scarlet smudge—brought back her shortness of breath, and with it the gnawing pain in her ribcage.

iii. Thoughts

WAS THERE enough money in the bank to pay the mortgage? The car payment? The kids' school tuition? What if her husband lost his job and they were forced to sell the house? What if he was cheating on her? What if she was too old to find anyone else? What if sea levels continued to rise? What if there were more droughts or famines? What if war broke out with Iran or North Korea? What if a tornado tore through their house? What if the children neglected to make good on their early promise? What if they squandered the opportunities she'd provided them and became addicts or criminals? What if one of them became sick? What if there was a shooting at school? What if all of life's covenants failed to be honored? What if the sun failed to shine? Would there be only the cold and dark?

iv. Mission

ACTION ALWAYS quelled these psychic insurgencies. She folded clothes. She dusted. She collected the laundry. She cleaned the coffee maker, wiped down the counters, swept the floors.

She prepared the children's breakfast. She prided herself in the speed and efficiency with which she completed this task, fine-tuned over seven years as a mother. Her ingredients were only the best: fresh, organic, and free of preservatives. She had become an adept at the art of ingredient-reading. The fine print, after decades of decoding the backs of cans and boxes, had given over its secrets to her.

She set their plates before them. Their little eyes stared up at her, wanting, needing. It broke her heart, knowing that they couldn't remain ignorant of life's sorrows. She hoped to keep this knowledge from them for as long as was ethical. But how long was too long?

The flip side was a kind of bestiality—their noses ran, their hands seethed with bacteria, their hair was a jungle in need of taming. She was a missionary, a deliverer of civilization. Before news of the world's genuine nature reached them, they needed to be brought to a place of acceptance.

She thought of her first child, a miscarriage, and the years of heartache that ensued. To feed these little ones, to put food on their plates, was itself a gift.

v. Seatbelts

SHE ADJUSTED and readjusted her son's seatbelt. She made sure the clasp lined up with his armpits. She withdrew her head from the car's shielded interior and glimpsed the sky: eighty degrees in February, chem-trails like cat's claws, a smell in the air like that of a morgue.

She turned the radio up loud to launch a singalong. She drove, obeying every law. She rehearsed in her mind the school's drop-off protocol. In the parking lot, she unbuckled the twins and combed their hair. She looked in her boy's eyes, examined his nose, checked his ears for wax. She clawed a small boulder of dried mucus from his nostril. She sniffed his breath. She returned to his hair, disheveled because of his cowlick. She smoothed it and it sprang back up. She pressed it down again with a lick of saliva.

As she held the children's hands and led them through the bustling halls, she thought she noticed a change in the other mothers' faces. There were more placid smiles than usual. There was a quieter look in their eyes, a wan acceptance like that of sleepwalkers.

"What's with everybody?" she said under her breath.

Once they were inside and the bell had rung, she returned to her car and listened to her heartbeat. Was it speeding up? She fished her bottle of baby aspirin from the glove compartment and swallowed four pills dry, then closed her eyes.

"Are you okay?" Cynthia said, materializing at her car window.

"You scared me."

"You look like you're freaking out."

"I'm fine."

"Can I come around?" Cynthia asked, pointing to the empty passenger seat. She thought of Cynthia's shoes, and the bacteria on their soles, and how they would end up on her car's mat, transferred to one of their feet, and ultimately invading her home.

"I'll come out instead," she said.

Cynthia put a gloved hand under her arm and led her to a bench by the baseball diamond. There was that smell in the air again, a portentous, sulfuric stench that seemed to blanket everything. She thought of the melting ice caps, the humongous underground caverns that, iced over for eons, were now belching something terrible into the gulf stream. She visualized the moon, and the solar system, and the infinite expanse beyond.

"Here," Cynthia said, shoving a business card into her hand.

"What's this?"

"A new doctor in town. A new pill."

"But Cynthia—"

"I know how you feel about pharmaceuticals. But this is different. All the mothers are on it."

She looked out across the lot. Women wearing beatific smiles drifted toward Mercedes, BMWs, Range Rovers. She remembered her son's piece of sticking-up hair. What if it had already sprung back? What misfortune would result? One taunt from a bully could send him hurtling down a path toward ruin.

A knot tightened in her stomach. She realized she hadn't eaten. But the prospect of food nauseated her. It made her think of her mouth, her esophagus, organs compressing and distending. This line of thinking branched out to her blood vessels, her lungs, her heart, and the slight lump she'd found in her breast two weeks ago in the shower, the one she'd been ignoring ever since.

"Trust me. The results are phenomenal."

"Thanks," she said, watching Cynthia drift off into the blossoming sun.

vi. Room

IN THE basement, she pried at the plaster, and it came away in damp nuggets. She tossed the larger pieces into a trash bag and vacuumed the smaller bits up with her German-made vacuum cleaner, one that she'd extensively researched in online forums. Sometimes she felt a deep love for the vacuum—a more expansive one than she even had for her children. It was the affection one could only have for an inanimate object with its tooled surfaces, pristine curves, precision manufacturing.

Once she removed enough of the plaster, she shined her phone's light into the crevice. Inside, she could make out a shallow crawlspace. It appeared to extend beyond the hole for several feet. Because of the opening's location under a knot of pipes, she couldn't get a good view. But the smell here was even more putrid, like a warning from another world.

vii. Pain

THE PAINS in her chest began two days later, in the shower, after probing the lump, as she'd done every morning for weeks.

The odor from the hole in the basement had made its way up the stairs, up through the heating ducts, to infect the upper floor of the house.

As she toweled herself off, the pain worsened into a red-hot soreness underneath her ribcage, as if she'd been kicked by steel-tipped boots. With each breath, it intensified, and her breathing grew short, spasmodic.

Her husband wouldn't be home until after the kids' bedtime. Tomorrow, he'd leave before any of them woke. To think of him was akin to contemplating a cardboard cutout. She experienced him chiefly as a series of traces: a whiff of aftershave, a cigar butt in the ashtray in the yard, an empty glass of scotch in the sink in the morning. She couldn't remember the last time they touched each other. For a moment she was gripped by the notion that she was a single mother, and he just a fantasy.

viii. Doctor

THE CLINIC was in a desolate corner of an anonymous corporate plaza at the edge of town. Dull, amber-glassed buildings zigzagged among browning trees. As she walked toward unit #236, she noticed there were no other cars in the lot.

Inside, reproduction artwork graced the beige walls. The receptionist took down her name and handed her a clipboard with paperwork. She retreated to one of the worn mauve chairs. The room smelled of rubbing alcohol and stale coffee. Somewhere in the building, someone was vacuuming. The sound set her at ease.

The questionnaire wasn't what she was expecting:

1. How often do you think about your own mortality?

2. On a scale of one to ten, how in touch are you with your own sexuality?

3. If you were told the world would end tomorrow, what would you do?

4. How often do you masturbate?

5. Are you averse to certain foods?

6. What do you feel is the meaning of life?

She answered the questions as honestly as she could. By the time she had arrived at the ultimate question—If given a knife and legal immunity, who in your life would you kill?—she was experiencing the soreness in her ribcage again. The pain spread its tentacles around to her spine, up her neck, and into the base of her skull.

A dwarfish woman in a black smock entered and called her name. She rose and followed her into a narrow fluorescent-lit hallway. Halfway down the hall, on a tall imitation wood pedestal, sat a bleached human skull.

"This way, ma'am," the woman said and motioned for her to enter a dank sitting room. A lamp with a stained-glass shade barely illuminated the interior. There were none of the standard trappings: no mechanical bed covered in tissue paper, no tongue depressors in jars, no equipment for checking vitals. Aside from the chair in which she sat, the only other thing in the room was a small television monitor.

She sat and waited, listening to muffled talk from beyond the door. She thought of the kids at school. Every day it was a struggle for her to surrender control, to let them out into the world, with its irrational undertows. If she could only have them here, now, in her arms.

A knock on the door. A youthful, handsome doctor entered. He had gray eyes vaulted by wispy blond eyebrows, a regal nose, a geometric jaw. Deep creases ran the course of his cheeks and forehead. She looked at his hands. A plain gold band hugged his ring finger. Then she saw that arthritis gnarled his fingers; he wasn't as young as he appeared at first glance.

"Hello, I'm Doctor Handy. What can we do for you today?" he asked with a theatrical smile. As he spoke, he flipped through her paperwork and scribbled notes in the margins. He didn't look her in the eyes.

"I've been having these pains, here, under my ribs. Shortness of breath. Indigestion. But I haven't been eating well. There's so little time, I have two children—twins—and—"

"Tell me, are you experiencing any symptoms as we speak?"

"Yes."

"It says here you never have thoughts of mortality. Is this true?"

"Not really."

"And you do not masturbate?"

Her face grew feverish. She pictured the doctor undressing her, pushing her up against the wall. What would his breath smell like? Garlic? Autumn leaves?

"I would like to run a test."

"Will it hurt?"

"It depends on how you define pain, and what your tolerance for it is. I will leave the room. That screen you see there will turn on. You will be shown a series of images. After a time, the images will cease. I will return to the room. Is this clear?"

"Yes."

"Now, may you please take your top off."

"My top?"

"Yes."

She unbuttoned her blouse and stripped down to her bra. The doctor placed a series of ice-cold electrodes on her chest, where they hung like the suckers of a mechanical squid. He adjusted the wires, switched on a small device to which the electrodes' wires were attached, and disappeared, trailing a scent of rotten eggs.

The small monitor in the corner came to life. Unspeakable images flashed across its glowing surface: a vivisected corpse on a morgue table, leaking viscera; a bruised body spilling from the window of a crashed vehicle; a pile of skeletal remains taken from a WWII newsreel; a dog with bloody fangs tearing at a piece of meat; a close-up view of a woman's genitals as she masturbated. The program lasted only a few minutes, and then the screen switched off.

The door opened, and the doctor came back. "Tell me," he said, "how do you feel?"

ix. Pill

She finished folding laundry. She made the beds, making sure the corners were razor sharp. She ran a damp cloth along the baseboards. She took everything out of the refrigerator, cleaned the glass shelves, checked all the use-by dates. She dumped and tossed the expired items' containers into the recycling bin. The rest she carefully placed back on their shelves, arranging them in rigid categories: condiments, sauces, dairy products, deserts.

There was still an hour before she had to pick the kids up at school. She stood at the kitchen window and thumbed the small prescription bottle.

THANATIN©, 50MG. DOSAGE: ONE PILL, ONE TIME ONLY.

She shook the bottle and the tiny black tablet hopped like a jumping bean. She filled her glass with triple-filtered water and swallowed it without a second thought.

x. Necropolis

AT THE corner of Seventh and Greenview, she noticed him—a man, worms fibrillating in his eye sockets, shambling toward her. She screamed and slammed on the gas, swerving into oncoming traffic and tearing across front yards, racing west. On the divider, a bed of flowers wilted in a black wave. Lawns turned to straw in pulsing swaths. Paint peeled from houses as they sagged and grew dark.

At the intersection, more animated corpses lurched with mocking grins: women, children, pets; blue-gray skin, dead eyes, mouths stuffed with rotten leaves. Her heart hammered. She reached into the glove compartment for her baby aspirin but found an empty bottle. Clouds swirled, and the sky blackened. Trees withered in time-lapse. A torrent of blood fell from the cracking sky and ran bubbling in the sewers.

The dead had overrun the school. Children with skin like moldering paper ran into the arms of grinning cadavers. Tornadoes of pestilence blew through the playground. Her heart raged against all she was seeing.

"You took it, didn't you, you devil?" a voice said. "Don't fret, it's intense, but once it wears off—not a worry in the world."

She turned to see Cynthia. A chunk of flesh fell from her friend's cheekbone into her lap. Rotten teeth tapped at the window. She tried to answer, but only a scraping groan came from her throat.

The twins bounced down the sidewalk. Death swirled around their festering heads, their blistering skin, their rotting clothes. "Get in!" she screamed.

"What's wrong?" her boy said, a toothless talking skull.

"We've got to get out of here."

"Why?" her little girl asked, skin sagging from her small bones and slopping like a pumpkin's innards onto the car seat.

"You're acting crazy," her boy said.

The assistant principal lumbered toward the window. As she put the car into reverse and screeched away, his bearded head fell from atop his leaking body and landed like a cabbage in the gutter.

xi. Demon

THE GARAGE door clamped out the light. Bryan's Porsche was there, engine ticking. He was never home this early. The twins cried in the back seat. She sat in the dark and listened to her pulse.

"I've seen it," she said.

"What?" her boy asked.

"It, in all its glory."

"You're scaring me," her girl said.

"Thank God you're both alive," she said. "Or are you?"

"Why is Daddy home so early?" her boy asked. She could

hear the shuffle and groans of the dead coming from outside the garage.

"Get in the house," she said.

Her husband was out of eyeshot, in the living room. She heard the clink of ice in a glass. "What's wrong?" his voice said.

"Why are you home?" she called.

I lost my job. I'm having an affair. I'm leaving you.

"I got done early today," he gurgled. Something about his voice sounded wrong. She heard his feet thump and drag towards them.

"Don't come near me!" she screamed.

Then he was slouching in the doorway. There was almost nothing left of him but bones. Inside his ribcage a few baggy organs drooped like old party balloons. "Get away!"

"Whoah, easy," he said.

"I want a divorce!" she screamed.

"Wait, hold on a minute—"

"Time is running out for me, do you understand? There is so much I want, so much I need, so much I deserve."

He laughed and came rattling toward her, teeth falling and skittering on the kitchen tiles. She swatted at him with her purse and he crumpled. Vertebrae clinked like dominoes. She turned to the children and watched as the rest of their contused skin sloughed off their bones into jellied heaps on the floor. She ran, pulled along on the scent of death to the basement.

The hole had gotten bigger; the pipes were disassembled. A bucket of standing water sat in the corner and a heap of plaster was piled against the far wall. She had no memory of the work she'd done here; it must have been after taking the pill. The odor permeated the room. Through the window, the world shriveled. Crimson rain fell in torrents. Great clumps of dead earth were sucked into the sky.

On all fours, she crawled into the hole. She realized the smell was not only coming from inside, but also from her body: the stench of eternal decay. A low animal growl began to issue from her throat.

In the dark, in the corner, she saw it, lying in a fungal heap: a dead mouse, feet upturned, mouth a rictus of pain. Maggots danced a ritual around its corpse. She gathered the small body into her arms. All the hurt she'd struggled to contain rose like a flood.

There was no mystery at the heart of nature, only this. The miniature corpse turned in her arms like the wheel of a slot machine. All fortune was poor fortune, she knew now, and for this knowledge she would be grateful. The fetus looked up at her and asked forgiveness. Don't blame yourself, we all go here, it said.

In the dark, she could see the twins reflected in its eyes. She saw her husband there, too, bound in his own way to terrible finiteness. And she recognized herself, one day to die, and because of this, beautifully alive.

"Mom, are you coming out of there?" she heard her boy ask.

"Honey, come on out," her husband said, with a laugh.

And then her girl, with the voice not of an angel, but of a human being, said, "Mommy, I'm hungry."

SUPER AWESOME THING

GRADY BRINGS it home from the birthday party in a goodie bag—all the kids got one. "Isn't it cool?" he asks. I look at the thing in his spidery hands. It makes a mammalian noise as he strokes its artificial skin. He gives it a hug, and it pulses like an internal organ. I notice the boy is strangely docile; he usually returns from parties having eaten too much cheap cake, hopped-up as if on amphetamines.

"So, what is it?" I ask.

"It's awesome."

"Isn't it wonderful?" Eliza asks, coming into the room. I am ironing my shirt, and the iron hisses.

"I don't know what it is, but I'm glad he had a good time," I say.

"Don't be so negative."

"How am I being negative?"

"You could show some interest," she says.

"Excuse me?"

"Grady, let's go. Your dad's in one of his moods."

When I peek in on them later, they are sitting in Grady's room with shades drawn staring at the thing. Eliza turns it over, pets it, passes it to Grady. I believe I see Grady whisper something into the thing's ear. Does it have an ear?

Eliza does not acknowledge my presence. It is not like her to shun me.

Just then Carmen wakes from her nap. I go into her room and draw the blinds. At first, she cries, but then quiets, which is is odd—she usually wails until I pick her up. I look down into her crib and see one of the things fibrillating in her chubby hands.

"Oh, you have one too," I coo. "She has one too?" I yell to the other room.

"I picked it up for her at the drugstore," Eliza says from Grady's room. "It was the last one. They were fighting over it in the car."

Carmen caresses the thing with her grubby fingers. It shines in the womblike light. Above her crib, on the shelf I installed before she was born, marches a column of dusty toys: wooden blocks, puzzles, a rainbow-colored stack of rings. I take a block down and try to pry the thing from the child's hands and replace it with the block, but she screeches and grips it tighter.

From somewhere in the house, I hear Grady say to his thing, "You are so super awesome."

For the rest of the afternoon, everybody sits alone playing furtively with their things. I read the newspaper: an airport lobby shooting, a supervirus, deportations, drone strikes. Dioxane plumes creep underground and forest fires burn. I wonder if this is how life will be like from now on, a hit parade of anxieties, a future in perpetual collapse.

At some point I drift off. I wake with the paper strewn at my feet. The house is reticent. I stand and stretch at the bay window. Grady, Carman and Eliza are in the backyard, as still as statues in the afternoon sun, staring skyward, where a trio of the objects flutter against the milk-white clouds.

AT WORK on Monday morning Clive calls me into his office. One of the things sits on his desk, purring. "You've got one too," I say.

"There's plenty behind you on the sofa," Clive says. "Grab whichever you want."

I turn to see a cardboard shipping box, flapped mouth gaping, vomiting twenty or thirty of the things across the calico cushions.

"They came from Agalma this morning," Clive says, tapping at his device's screen.

"Agalma?"

"Agalma, Inc. The client. They make the things. Well, they design them; they're manufactured in Shenzhen. They need us to put together a crisis package for the product. The typical menu items. Website, community outreach, social media. I'd jump right into the holding statement. They don't want to waste any time."

"What kind of crisis?"

"Crises. Seems as though there've been a host of adverse effects."

"Such as?"

"Let's see… bedwetting with children, a suicide. Five people have been shot outside of a Walgreens in Florida. A class action suit concerning microwave radiation. And supplies are running low. There's talk of rioting in the Midwest."

"I'm confused."

"About?"

"I don't even know what these things do."

Clive twirls his thing around in his manicured fingers. He looks up from it and laughs. "Are you losing it Marcus?"

"I think I require some knowledge of a product before I defend it publicly on behalf of the firm."

"Have you had your coffee yet? Grab yours from the box and come back to me with a plan by tomorrow. At the very least, I need a holding statement by COB."

ON THE way to my office, I pass Buck's desk. He's sitting with his feet up, tossing one of the things up and catching it backhanded. "Yo," he says, not looking at me. He has a postcoital gaze in his eyes.

"Listen, Buck—"

"I'm not listening. Just kidding."

"I've been told we've been engaged by a company called Agalma?"

"And?"

"Well, Clive has me on it. I don't even know what these things are."

"They're amazing, is what they are."

"Yeah, but—"

"Did you ever dream of some… thing? And when you wake, you can feel it in your hands? Like it's a piece of you that's been missing all your life?"

"Yes. No. Maybe."

Just then Buck's phone chimes. "I have to take this, Marcus," he says. "My wife's trying to track down some for the kids, but everyone's sold out."

I SPEND the day online, gathering info. The things are being marketed under various brand names. This strikes me as odd for a new patent-pending product; usually this happens only after a company's trademark lapses. The pricing is wildly different as well: some net retailers are selling them for as little as $2.99; others for upwards of two hundred bucks.

I exchange emails with Garth Milo, Agalma's in-house spokesperson. The messages are terse, informational, riddled with grammatical glitches. I suspect Milo might be a bot. I decipher that he is awaiting our firm's issuance of a holding statement, which he'll present to the public. He wants to know our social media strategy, and would like a write-up before we introduce any campaigns via various platforms.

I click around Agalma's website. It appears hastily constructed, rife with typos and broken links. No phone numbers are provided. Although they list several global locations on their contact page, the company is headquartered in Giles, only twenty minutes by car.

Things move fast in PR. I am used to having cases dumped on me last minute. But I am at a loss. By the time five o'clock rolls around, my statement is still a blinking cursor on my screen. I watch my colleagues file past, cradling and stroking their things. Each one of them has the look of a cloudless summer day. As they jibe and shove each other like playground children, I grow jealous. Soon the office goes empty and dark and I fall asleep at my keyboard.

I dream of a large object in my hand. It is dense, like a minor planet. I realize it isn't the object that's huge, but that I'm a small child. The object has been presented to me as a gift on an unnamed occasion. There are no Christmas trees or birthday cakes, only a ring of smiling adults, their faces hazy, their voices garbled. Happiness spreads through me and bleeds out onto a spiritual plane. When I wake, my heart feels swollen. I look at the hair on the back of my hands and nearly cry for what I've lost.

I remember the box on Clive's sofa; I'd forgotten to take one of the things with me as I left our meeting. I go to his office, but the door is locked. I scour the cubicles, the kitchen, the storeroom, but cannot find any of the things.

On my way out, I stop by the lounge. A few minutes in the comfy chair, after-hours, has become a ritual. A bit of TV clears out my glitches like the tip of a paperclip pressed into the reset button of an electronic device.

The candidate is holding a press conference. It's two months after the nomination and the world is still dazed. Darnell Hayes, mass murderer—in defiance of all opinion polls—is running a successful presidential campaign via social media from his cell on death row.

When Hayes first announced his run, the country erupted in lazy protest. Lawsuits were brought, legal scholars blogged, pundits bared their fangs. Eliza, sallow and dry-mouthed, organized. She bought poster board for picket signs. She typed frantic messages to neighborhood mothers. For weeks her face remained tightened into the rictus of an Olympic weight-lifter in mid-press.

I've always been cynical about politics: it's all a shitshow. But my wife takes up causes like orphaned children. She had lawn signs printed, T-shirts made, buttons stamped. Her phone pinged at all hours. She shaved her head, took to angry exercise, stopped attending yoga.

I watched this all with amusement. There was no way they would elect Hayes. Despite decades of creeping apathy and lowering voter turnout, Americans still had some decency left. Yes, binge-watching had sapped most of the citizenry's capacity for critical thought, but deep down we were all human. Weren't we?

The NEXT morning, I make an excuse at the office—Grady is sick and I need to pick him up at school—and I ride out to the Agalma headquarters in Giles. The place is at the far end of a winding corporate drive, home to anonymous industrial-age businesses with names like Propeon Inc. and Dynaclear Solutions. What any of these places sold, or produced, was anybody's guess.

The Agalma building is a squat, bricky affair with gloomy, tinted windows. I ring the bell and no one answers. I hop through the glossy bushes and head round back, peering inside as I go: computer equipment, wires snaking like arteries, but no desks and no chairs and not a soul in sight.

I ask around. A receptionist at the tool-and-die shop next door says she'd never seen anyone come or go. "I get a weird feeling about the place," she says. "We don't go near it. I hear things."

"What kind of things?" I ask.

"Funny things," she whispers.

On my way to the car, I hear an insectoid buzz overhead. One of the things floats above the treetops, darting back and forth like a clockwork hummingbird. I drive home, taking a circuitous route. For a while, the thing trails me, but eventually I lose it.

PEOPLE STOP showing up for work. Meeting attendance is made optional. Clive, ordinarily rage-prone, appears unfazed.

I turn in a rather late and lazy crisis package, and he has little to say on either its quality or tardiness.

Our staff of designers and technologists deploy the campaign, and we monitor public opinion. It seems Agalma has made software updates which may have mitigated some of the more harmful side effects, though it is hard to tell. Horror stories proliferate, some real, some imagined.

Demand rises; stocks are depleted. The National Guard is called into port cities to safeguard Agalma shipments from Shenzhen. Rogue capitalist militia groups have been hijacking shipping containers and selling the things on the black market. Jailbroken devices show up on the dark web, modified to induce trancelike states, multiple orgasms, inter-dimensional travel.

At home, Eliza has stopped eating. I try to talk to her. She takes her thing into another room and sits talking with it, the way we once did, years ago, when we first found each other. I make a plea for less thing-time, more people-time, but she only rolls her eyes and assumes a fetal position.

Part of this seems a prophecy fulfilled. For years I've felt the rather tenuous connection between us has been in danger of evaporating. There is too much pressure in the world, too many distractions. I've tried to keep my family together, focused on what matters most, but the forces that gather beyond the walls are too strong to fend off alone.

We get a call from school that Grady's grades are tanking. I agree to meet with the principal. When I arrive, I find her in her office fiddling with one of the things. With a faraway look in her eyes she says, "There is exciting recent research to suggest that more free play is beneficial to a child's development."

I can't get anything more out of her. I leave her in her trance and stalk the halls. Kids are petting their things, placing them inside their lockers, spray painting murals of them in the parking lot. Agalma's cheery logo has appeared on soda machines, lunch boxes, shaved into one child's purple-dyed hair. In the parking lot, I watch two teenage girls get catty over one of the things. By the time I'm in the car, the altercation has devolved into hair-pulling and biting.

On my way out of the lot, I pass the school security guard's cruiser. I roll down my window and peer inside. He's in the back seat, in full uniform, curled up asleep with a pulsing thing in his arms.

Two months drift by, and it's Election Day. But all anyone wants to talk about are the Super Awesome Things—a major announcement about version 2.0 is imminent. It seems our work at the firm was a success. Despite ongoing violence and a slew of newly discovered ill effects—depression, financial ruination, skyrocketing addiction—Agalma's public image is spotless. Third-quarter earnings have exceeded all market projections. People go to the polls, but what they are most interested in is the fact that Agalma is now the most profitable corporation of all time.

That night, to distract myself from the election results, I try to initiate sex with Eliza. She flops like a marionette. I get aggressive and she shoves me off. I give up and attempt to sleep. In the middle of the night, I check the news sites; Hayes is projected to win. I leave Eliza, asleep with her thing cuddled in her arms, and crawl into Grady's bed. I cry for what his future might hold.

The next morning, Eliza is chipper. She grinds coffee like a champion barista. Grady is flying his thing above his head from room to room. Carmen is dribbling in her high chair, petting her thing like a hamster.

"I can't believe it. Did you see?" I ask.

"See what?" Eliza says, spooning one tablespoon of refined sugar after another into her coffee. She rarely uses sugar in her coffee, and if she does, it's always the raw organic stuff. I can see she has her thing in her sweatpants pocket, where it glows like an active volcano.

"He won! What are we going to do?"

Just hearing myself say it out loud breaks something in me. I realize my cynicism has always been a buttress against a profound sense of approaching calamity. And here it was, and I was facing it alone.

"Dad, look what it can do!" Grady yells. His hand is inside the thing, and it is moving sluggishly up his arm. "Do you think I can get all the way inside?"

"Why don't you try?" Eliza says, sipping her sludgy coffee. "Or I tell you what, Gray, we can all try. It'll be awesome, won't it? Carmen, you and I will all try to go inside."

I call in sick to work, but decide to go—I need to get out. The streets are deserted. Here and there, abandoned cars sit with their doors open. I notice a few smashed shop windows. On the corner of Fifth and Wilson, a fight has broken out. The curb is red with gristle, as if someone has been smashing tomatoes.

The radio announcer says, "The nation has vowed to avenge the assassination of the cleric. Thousands mourned, chanting 'death to America.' In stock news, Agalma climbed over 94 percent in one day on the verge of its recent product announcement. Excitement on Wall Street and Main Street is at an all-time high. Holiday shopping season will start early this year."

The office is vacant. Papers litter the aisles; desks are overturned. Someone has pinned a large American Flag to the wall. Remnants of a fire are visible in the kitchen; the walls are charred and spattered with flame retardant.

On my way home, I stop by the pharmacy for my allergy medication. In the parking lot, I slump in the car, engine ticking, and look up at a street lamp. There is something beautiful about how its head glows against the purple-black sky. I close my eyes and press on my eyelids. I watch the phosphenes dance against a curtain of veins.

I am looking inside myself. Not in the usual philosophical sense, but literally. Within me a universe pulses. Stars live and die. Mighty oceans flow. All day long, we go about our petty business unaware of the cosmoses that turn inside us. We only stop to think about it when something goes wrong. Cancer spreads like dark matter through brain tissue. A bone cracks like a sun blinking out.

I open my eyes and notice a crowd has formed against the bright revolving doors of the pharmacy. An endless line of people snakes along the store's enormous brick wall. I get out of the car and weave my way through the throng. Some are waiting patiently; others stare into the haloes of their phones. People grow restless and begin to push and shove. A commotion erupts at the head of the formation. I hear a bottle smash, angry shouts. Out on the boulevard, cars honk and sirens wail.

I shoulder through the chaos into the store's fluorescence. Inside there is mayhem. Six dazed cashiers work frantically; there is usually only one. Displays have been overturned in protest. Smashed bottles of makeup and torn tissue boxes litter the aisles.

I grab my allergy meds and muscle my way to the front of the store, which has descended into pandemonium. There is a large cardboard box with the Agalma logo printed in bright colors on its sides. The crowd is tearing the box apart, but it is empty. A weeping child holds a decapitated doll in her arms. A man vaults the checkout counter. A woman follows. They pin a cashier against a wall of cigarette cartons. Then: a loud pop, a gunshot. Sparks rain down as a slender metal lighting fixture dislodges from the ceiling and swings in a great sputtering arc over our heads.

At home, the house is silent. Remnants of dinner litter the table. There are signs of a struggle—Carmen's spilled bottle, Grady's backpack exploded across the floor, Eliza's purse overturned, belching lip gloss and hairpins. "Hello?" I call, and no one answers. I drop onto the sofa. One of the Super Awesome Things throbs there, next to me. I pick it up and draw it close. It moves onto my finger, and the feeling is indescribable. I recall childhood days of ice cream and my mother's bright breath at night as she tucked me into bed. I think of all those small wonders, forever lost. As the world draws its last gasp, I go inside the thing, and I am happy.

THE MAN ON THE BENCH

THE PARK was a postage stamp atop a hill at the edge of town. Humming with insects, speckled with flowers, it invited visitors to wander delicate paths or picnic on lush lawns. The path leading to its center, where a gazebo stood awash in light, was neatly trimmed, abuzz with bees and laced with fragrances reminiscent of cinnamon and butterscotch. Here most of the neighborhood's sounds were filtered down to distant echoes. Maple leaves shimmered against the sky's cobalt dome. A freshly painted wrought-iron bench posed in the shade of a stately oak. This, I decided, was my favorite spot in the world. Here, I would take a book, or newspaper, and slip out of the day's rapids into the slow ocean of time.

WE HAD recently moved to the town, I and my lovely wife and two sparkling children. We agreed these were the happiest days of our lives. The first sight of our new home dispelled the fears associated with uprooting my family for a new position at a new firm: mowed lawns, beaming neighbors, a community calendar full of cultural events.

It wasn't long before we felt integrated. Our children won a lottery which gained them entrance to a progressive magnet school, my wife got a job at the local florist, designing bouquets for weddings and holidays, and I slipped into the rhythms of my new workplace. After a year of hard work, the firm made me partner. The future gleamed with potential.

I had never been much of a walker, and I seldom preferred to be alone, but within weeks of our arrival, the bright streets of the unfamiliar town called to me. My wife thought it odd when, one Saturday morning, I announced that I would go for a stroll.

"By yourself? That isn't like you," she said.

"What am I like?" I replied. I was young; I was still building a persona. A certain measure of autonomy was healthy. The children seemed disappointed when I walked out the door into the summer haze. But I told myself that solitude was restorative, and, besides, I needed to familiarize myself with our new surroundings.

THE FIRST time I encountered the park, I skirted its perimeter. Having moved from the city, it seemed meek, uninteresting. Towns across American were filled with places like this, injected into community planning as an afterthought. Often, they were derelict. Drifts of trash would collect against chain-link fences, weeds infested neglected corners, swing sets rusted in the rain.

But one morning I detoured through. The entrance lay at its southwest corner, where a bronze statue of a man atop a horse stood in the rising light. From a plaque beneath the monument, I learned this was F. Wilson White (1790-1862), the town's founder. White, a land speculator, had established the town on January 12th, 1892.

I moved on. As I passed through the gate, a feeling of contentment overcame me. Most of the afternoon slipped by without notice. By the time I returned home, evening had already fallen and my wife was incensed.

"You've been gone all day," she said.

"I lost track of time," I answered.

"This worries me," she said.

"There is nothing to worry about," I replied.

But she was correct: something was wrong. The park drew me in with its serenity, but like all perfect places, it contained a kernel of potential trauma. Something awful might happen there, and it was my duty to ward it off, or soak up the perfection before it passed.

As I made my way to the park, I'd often pass smiling neighbors, out walking dogs or pushing strollers. As was my inclination, I would make eye contact, inviting them wordlessly to walk with me. I yearned to exchange pleasantries with these unfamiliar people. Cynics often deride small talk, but for me, it was one of life's pleasures. Tiny sparks start large fires. A chance encounter, a conversation about the weather, could lead to a lifelong friendship.

I received a few smiles, nods of the head. Occasionally, a passerby would cast his or her eyes down at the sidewalk. Given how welcoming I found the neighborhood to be, this behavior was puzzling. But it was no bother: I was an unfamiliar face. Soon enough, I would be accepted.

My bench-sitting became a routine. The place called to me. It spoke the language of bird song and breezes, but also of tragic history and portents. Every Saturday morning, and well into the afternoon, I'd sit with my paper, with only the rasp of its pages as company. Several months passed, a period during which sometimes I never encountered another soul in the park.

Occasionally, a mother with a stroller would join me, cooing to her newborn, taking lunch on a bench further up the path.

I wondered about her husband. Was he a busy man, working on weekends? Did he command a high-powered position at a job even more rewarding than mine? I developed a connection with the woman, although we never spoke. We were joined by the park, and whenever she arrived, I felt an expectation. I sensed that a future event would somehow bind us together.

I waited to see what would happen.

It was only when the trees thinned, and a fall chill saddened the air, that I noticed the copse. At the far side of the park, opposite the statue, the central path became overgrown and rubbly and was soon swallowed by a patch of murky woods.

My time on the bench took on a slight discomfort once I noticed the trees. I would try to concentrate on my paper, but the copse, like a bit of dust lodged in the eye, refused to surrender my attention.

As autumn fell, and the leaves withered, a new view opened up: a grimy mausoleum of brick buildings that constituted a housing project. These monoliths stood brutal and uncaring at the edge of my vision. I turned my back to them, but they remained stubbornly visible. Even if I looked away, toward home, I could feel their weight on my back.

But even more than the buildings, it was the trees—wet with rot, void of light and air—that wouldn't leave my thoughts.

Over dinner, the family took notice of my reticence to engage in conversation. All I could see were the trees. I became less attentive to the house. Small areas of disrepair grew unmanageable. The faucet leaked; the toilets ran. The trees, and the housing project beyond them, siphoned all my pride. They came with me to bed at night and dripped into my dreams.

LIFE IS a tournament. You train, make mistakes, learn from them, and try again. You study the sport of living, drill yourself in its rules. You set out in the morning expecting the day's tribulations to bolster your perseverance. Perfection is the engine of life. But injuries are sustained, and sometimes they are permanent. There will be no silver medal. Glory doesn't just fade; occasionally it passes you altogether.

I had never thought this way, until now. Before my time in the park, I'd always held the most optimistic of world views. But the trees had spoken to me, and they said these words: you must come to terms with your lack.

My wife was right. A change was coming.

The trees commanded me to remove all the mirrors from the house. My wife came home one evening to find the medicine cabinets tossed out onto the curb; the floor-length bedroom mirror torn from its mounts and thrown in the garbage; the mirror on the nightstand smashed.

"What's happening to you?" she said, crying. "What have you done?"

"The trees, they told me to do it," I said.

I KEPT the trees out of mind as best I could. I inhaled the sweet scents of early autumn. I walked on the sun-dappled paths and knelt to pick through acorns. I searched for hours, one afternoon, for the perfect one: smooth, unblemished, with an unbroken cupule like an emperor's crown.

With my thumbnail, I pressed two smiling eyes and a beaming mouth into the nut's waxen flesh. A roar came from the trees. The sky darkened, clouds raced, the swings moaned. I trudged home in a thunderous rain, ashamed of what I'd done.

As I walked, people stared through screen doors, derision burning in their eyes. When I arrived home, I found the house desolate. Not only empty of my family, but of all signs they'd ever existed.

I found rotten food in the refrigerator, cigarette burns on the carpet. Trails of mud and wet leaves wound through the rooms. What looked like blood spattered the walls. Who, besides us, had been here? I sat on the worn sofa and stared through the window at the jeering storm.

The rain tapered, and the sun burst through the clouds. Once again, the park called to me. I left my broken home and raced through the streets.

I PUSHED through the park and into the trees. All around me were the sweet, sharp odors of decomposition. Mud caked my shoes. Decay bit at my nostrils. It was a smell that was intimately known to all of us, yet impossible to describe. I realized then what soil was: the death of everything, life brought from its bright vigor into black, sucking muck.

I pressed on. Twigs tore at my clothes, clawed at my skin. How long was I there? A change was coming over me, one the trees had warned about. A deep sleep, or perhaps an awakening. Like tiny fingers, the branches were holding me back.

I burst free and found myself at a chain-link fence. Beyond it rose the towers of the housing project. Graffiti blighted the walls. A burned-out car stood on blocks in the cracked street. A lone basketball hoop crouched against the heavy sky.

I recognized this place, and the shame that came with it. I was forbidden to leave; I was never to show my face in the park. Scared of getting caught, I scaled the fence and crossed the concrete grounds toward one of the brick buildings. An elevated highway roared above, and I sped under, through the trash and broken glass. In the space below the underpass, I found myself among a familiar pile of debris—crumbled asphalt, rusted metal, discarded clothes. I sifted through the garbage. I felt like I'd done this before, all my life perhaps.

The sun was setting somewhere behind concrete. Beyond the dead buildings, it spread its tattered blanket across a world that would soon be lost. The odors of exhaust, rotting trash, and burnt rubber welcomed me. A wild dog sniffed at the lip of a sewage tunnel. I caught myself in a shattered rearview mirror—a black-skinned face, split and doubled into a crowd of shadows. I picked up a piece of rusted metal. It looked like it had once been part of a car door, perhaps the mechanism which raised and lowered its window. It resembled the shape of a gun. I gripped it in my fingers. It felt good.

"I told you not to go down there!" I heard Momma shout.

I looked up, and there she was, as I'd always known her, inky face twisted with rage, her whole bitter life turning in her black marble eyes. I watched her crouch down and pick up something from the ground. She leaned back and cocked her arm, a beer bottle shining in her fist. She fired it down at me and it crashed against concrete. Green angry shards sung out. I felt a stab of pain in my head.

I ran.

Up the crumbling embankment, across the tired grass, and along the fence. I came to a hole and scraped through. I looked down and there was blood on my hands, my shirt.

I pounded back through the trees and plunged into the mud which sucked at my ankles. I dragged myself free, leaving a sneaker behind. I stood up and ran, and fell, and ran, and burst out of the trees into the park.

White faces all turned to stare. The mother yanked her stroller to a halt. It was growing dark. I looked at my hand, blacker than the night. It still clutched the gun-like piece of junk. How did my skin get this way? Had I spent too long in the dirt and in the mud? Could I ever wash it away?

"Don't move," I heard the police shout.

"Drop it," one of them roared, from across the park's darkening lawn.

The mother with the stroller screamed.

I lurched toward her, wanting to say Everything's okay. I know you. We are friends and neighbors, aren't we? I won't hurt you.

But it seemed I already had hurt her. Just by being there, I'd hurt her.

People dove to the ground. Two shots like thunder, and then two punches—in my chest and in my arm. Birds went pounding into the tumbling sky. The world swerved. Here I was again, I thought, face-down in the muck, among the trees. I could smell it, the place I came from and where I belonged. I looked back across the park. I saw the black leather shoes of the police, hammering toward me, soldierly and with terrible purpose. The mother beside the collapsed stroller, crying with her baby in her arms, the child's white skin translucent in the vanishing light.

As dark swept across my vision, I saw the man on the iron bench, with his newspaper. He looked like a lucky man: white-skinned, perfectly dressed, kind blue eyes locked on me. They were a father's eyes, a husband's eyes. I imagined his life;

it seemed the most perfect thing to do, a final flight to go be with him. As the life bled from me, I rose up and out over the grass, above their heads, sirens rising with me like a chorus of angels. I found the man on the bench and laid down inside him.

THE NOOK

THEY SAY man is a social animal. I have never liked to be around people, so perhaps I am not a man. Perhaps I am not even an animal.

Because of this, I have seldom fit in. I have spent my life moving from place to place. In the autumn of my forty-second year, I found myself in a gray midwestern town looking for somewhere to be. I'd been left money by a recently deceased great-aunt whom I'd never met. I saw this as a chance to abstract myself further from anything resembling social interaction. I'd quit my job and driven west with no one but myself as a companion.

I chose the town because of its emptiness. The streets, tangled near its interior, grew sparse on the outskirts, eventually pushing up against brambly fields and disused farmlands. The place was barely keeping wildness at bay.

I applied for an apartment in a housing complex located in just such a liminal space, where liquor stores and filling stations gave way to thorny brush and desolate lots. The development was composed of cracked looping driveways and squat Vietnam-era buildings that lay tomblike among the weeds. The agent—far too friendly—led me around the perimeter, reading from a script of amenities, rules, regulations. Each unit had its own balcony. Most were home to dead potted plants, sun-bleached rugs, rusted lawn chairs. I saw no people. I liked the place immediately.

My apartment—tiny, anemic, dusty—was located in a sublevel at the rear of building C. This structure—one of the oldest—was farthest from the office, and butted up against a dark patch of trees. The hallway was dank, the carpet stained. I was thankful that my unit had no windows. I encountered no neighbors, heard not a sound. It was as though I were the last person alive. I was overjoyed.

At the end of my apartment's hallway, beyond the stairwell and around a blind corner, was a small nook. This dim cinderblock alcove was empty except for spiderwebs and dead insects. It had no purpose that I could ascertain—no electrical boxes, light switches, storage closets—and therefore seemed to me a place where no one would ever have a reason to go. Instead of my apartment, which was blighted by the psychic residue of past occupants, I began to spend more time in the nook.

After becoming attuned to the space, I was able to pick up readings. I regressed down the years, exploring the nook's numinous record. As I peeled back the layers, I found no evidence of human presence. Farther, farther back I went, arriving in 1968, the year of the building's construction.

Still more forceful than the residues in my apartment, I felt the presence of the worker who had poured the cement, bricked the walls, but his aura was as diluted as a teardrop in an ocean. There was something troubling about this man, something I recoiled from. Riding below these currents, like a seismic tremor, was another manifestation, something I couldn't pinpoint. It didn't present itself as a presence but as an absence. My mind fled from this erasure like a startled bird.

Pressing farther back, I sensed only the crosshatched travails of native peoples, frontiersmen, animals. I reached inside and swept these traces away with my mind's broom. Into history's dustpan they went, like fingernails, dead leaves, iron filings.

THE NOOK was a place of near-perfect loneliness, but my presence was weakening this aura. Therefore, once a day I'd make it a point to leave and adventure aboveground. I'd walk out across the dry reedy grounds of the complex. At their far end, among sun-choked grass, I came upon an abandoned school. I found a broken window in the cafeteria that I used to gain entrance. Years of graffiti laced the walls. The ghosts of children scurried by my feet, late to class, late to life. So much hurt in those halls, so much worry. My own formative years came back to me in the sonorous gymnasium, with its cracked floor and rusted hoop. If all the world is a stage, this was mine. My voice's echoes met no one's ears but my own, and I was alive.

ALL MY life I've been drawn to the lonely places. I've made it a point to see and categorize them all—the places we've razed, paved, built upon, and abandoned. The underpasses, cathedrals of rubble, stinking of urine and exhaust. The industrial driveways, pocked with grease stains. The narrow fissures between storage containers. Expressway shoulders peppered with shards of glass and sunbaked peels of rubber.

Once, when I was fourteen, behind a boarded-up refilling station, I slept aside a rusted Dumpster and dreamt that it swallowed the whole world of things and men and me along with it.

On my seventh night in the nook I discovered the egress. I

had moved my bedding into the nook, along with a few books and other supplies. I had purchased a bag of white bread and lunch meat at the liquor store across the highway. I always chose mass-produced products, as my antennae went dead around them—they seldom came into contact with human hands, only machines.

To celebrate the discovery of the nook, I had also purchased a small bottle of rye whiskey, which the clerk took from the shelf behind the counter and placed in a plastic bag. I reached inside the bag to extract the bottle, and a warm jolt shot up my fingertips. The evidence of all those who had touched the bottle, on its journey from manufacture to sale, jumped through me like an injection. As if having grabbed a hot pan from a stovetop, I flung the bottle into the corner of the nook where, instead of shattering, it vanished.

I FOUND the bottle, intact, in one of the lockers inside the school. The door had long gone unhinged; the shelves were bent into rusty chevrons. I studied the bottle in the shifting light. The children danced at my feet: too much pain, too much joy. I raised my fingertip to the bottle's amber skin and brought it near. Nothing. I curled my hand around it, and my antennae remained cold. All remnants had been cleansed from it, like water spots from a window.

I PASSED more objects through. Each materialized in the locker bleached of human touch. A plastic comb I found in an abandoned lot. A dog's leash I discovered tied to a post. A pair of discarded underwear. An empty pack of cigarettes. A broken bicycle pump. Each arrived from its journey pristine,

sterling, washed with inhuman light. That night in the nook, I
cried tears of joy. I had discovered what I had been seeking all
my life: a doorway to pure desolation.

When I was twelve years old, he cornered me at the bicycle
rack behind school. I had been late leaving, and the grounds
were already empty of children. It was just the two of us. He
knocked me down onto my knees and pushed my head into
the gravely soil. Stones cut into my face, bringing blood. I
couldn't breathe.

How long did he hold me there, with his saliva falling in
loops across my face? I had never experienced pain like that—a
deep eternal hurt that went up and out of me across the bleachers,
bursting into the air with the blackbirds, too much for my small
body to contain. I cried and my tears muddied the soil. Night
fell on me as I walked home, and has never lifted.

I avoided the bicycle rack from that point on. The place was
cursed, soured by what had happened between us. Every day
you pass a place like this, a locus where too much hurt has bled
through the fabric of the universe, leaving behind an unfading
stain that is capable of bending time and space, a black hole
that feeds on anguish and lets no light escape.

I prepared myself as one would prepare a body for a burial.
I bathed, groomed, put on my only suit. In the dark nook I lit
three candles. I thought of everyone I had known, all those that
had heaped upon me shame, derision, guilt. Each encounter, a
stain upon my life's white page. How many years had I longed
to be rinsed of these things? To be standing on the precipice
of this power was like being a saint before God.

At midnight I stepped toward the nook's dark shining corner. Three angles' convergence, cement, gray latex paint—dead manufactured things, arranged in such a way as to open a door to a place free of life, death, and everything in between.

I jumped. It was like falling through cold water. Time ceased its endless pull. I was suspended in darkness.

I SEE a child, a young girl, in ribbons and a paisley dress. The bell rings and she spins the tumbler on her locker's lock. Children—familiar to me in their scents and thoughts and dreams—stream past like fish. She has never seen pain, or humiliation. She deposits her books—sparkly stickers, hearts like soaring birds, phone numbers of friends and crushes—into the locker's warm mouth. It smells of bubblegum and hairspray. She drifts through the crowd toward the faceted sun.

A man—the construction worker—stands off in the field, watching. He has recently returned from another world. He's seen villages burned, infants set on fire, corpses strung from rafters like sides of beef. Among the majestic grass's blades, he steals her, out across the sky and underground. He takes her through the labyrinth, as if returning her to the womb. It smells of fresh paint, plaster, sawdust. In the dark he rips at her dress. A tear slips through tangled limbs, detonating like ordnance in the nook's cold corner. A hole is torn in the world's weak skin. On the other side I float, waiting to be erased of not only my pain, but everyone's.

THE STORE

i. Magazine

It is hard to say how long we've been in the store. None of us can remember. When I first arrived, a dark electric sky threatened rain. Since then, we've watched the clouds come and go like crowds at a station. Sometimes, it seems as though it was only yesterday since I first came; other times it feels like an eternity.

It has been two days since our last escape attempt. Davis at the magazine rack organized the debacle. Ever since, he has been despondent, buried in Good Housekeeping. I've tried to get through to him. I make the excuse that I'm browsing the paperbacks in order to see how he's doing. He seems to be leaving us. Perhaps it is for the best.

ii. Lipstick

I continue my rounds. I stop by the makeup aisle to talk to Shawna. She has a tube of lipstick and is drawing a diagram of the store's layout on the linoleum. Empty tubes litter the floor. Her fingertips are stained crimson, as if she's been dissecting corpses.

"Any luck?" I ask.

"Yeah right," she says.

"That's a nice color."

"It's called Rouge Rapture."

I look over her shoulder. Corridors snake in and out of each other. Arrows point into and out of dead ends. Question marks float in the center of blurry voids. She wipes a quadrant of the map away with her sleeve and begins again. On the floor beside her are several wallet-size photographs: her son, Mitchell; her husband, Eddie; her mother, Pearl.

"Well, anyway. Let me know how it goes."

"I guess," she says, opening a bag of crinkle-cut chips. By the Cheetos end cap I glance back, and see that her face is buried in her hands.

iii. Laundry Basket

I DRIFT through the bright plentitude. I ride the air conditioner's currents. I make it a point to avoid the toy aisle, as it reminds me too much of my daughter Jenni. Like Shawna, I may never see my family again, and anything to prevent such a thought has become part of my survival strategy. I cut through electronics and make my way to the warehouse, where I've set up quarters. Armand sits in the seat of the forklift, smoking and reading The Enquirer.

"Jesus was spotted at a mall in Georgia."

"Shopping?"

"He was in the food court."

"He was eating?"

"Maybe he was just hoping to be seen."

"Do you have to do that around here?" I say, waving the smoke out of my face.

"What's the difference?"

"It's bad for you is the difference."

"We're all screwed anyway."

"Are you giving up?"

"Maybe."

I make my bed—an inflatable mattress and fine thread count sheets—and head off down one of the towering aisles to look for Shane. When I find him, he is throwing a basketball into a laundry basket that he's clamped to one of the shelves' thick metal beams. Shane is our youngest, only twelve. His mother sent him to the store to buy toilet paper, and he's been with us ever since.

"What are you doing?" I ask.

"What does it look like?"

"How are you doing?"

"I don't know."

"You know we will get out of here, right? One day, you'll see your mother again."

He lets the ball bounce away into the shadows and turns to me. His eyes are like a gerbil's. There is so much love in the world, and yet we tend to keep it from each other. I walk up and put my arms around him. He backs away, but then relents. Among the powdered beverages and lithium-ion batteries, we hug.

iv. Ibuprofen

DEBORAH HAD sent me to buy ibuprofen for the baby. It was the middle of the night, so my only choice was the 24-hour place on Plainview. I left them there, my two lovely ones, in the powdery glow of the sky-and-clouds nightlight, humidifier coughing mist, with Jenni, hot as a baked potato, crying in Deb's arms.

I said, "I'll be right back," which I now know was a lie, or if not a lie, then definitely untrue. If they had only known that my secret wish was to leave and never come back—not because I didn't love them, but because the responsibility often threatened to crush me like an avalanche.

v. Candy

THE FIRST escape attempt was coordinated by Ron the Cashier. Those were the early days, when hope still graced the halls of our fluorescent prison. Ron knew the place better than any of us. We huddled as a team in the beverage aisle, reflected like dancers in the panes of the refrigerated shelves. Ron explained that the temporary display of Halloween items that obscured the front door could be circumvented by penetrating a narrow row of creepy props and plastic pumpkins. He seemed to have it all figured out. His confidence was electrifying.

We went single file past the masks and costumes. A vampire leered. A motion-activated werewolf howled. A zombie's plastic hand brushed Shawna's wrist and she screamed. I jumped back into a display. Candy corn scattered across the floor like beetles. Armand slipped and went plowing through a cardboard Frankenstein's monster. Davis screamed, fooled by the cutout's realism, and fainted into the shelves, which upended, teetered, and came crashing down on my shin.

"I was wrong," Ron said, shaking his head. His name tag was smeared with chocolate. The tag said Hello my name is Ronaldo I'm happy; the "to help you" had been scraped off ages ago, a remnant of his days when he still came to work with the certainty that he'd leave at the end of his shift.

"What do you mean?" I said, pulling my foot out from under a huge plastic spider.

"I thought the slight brightening beyond the graveyard was a way out, but it isn't."

We all stood and looked out across the debris. He was right; it wasn't an exit, only a window that looked out onto the gray asphalt, the lights like wire hangers, the yellow faded lines like a child's drawing. The trees coughed, the interstate beyond them just a thin gleaming ribbon in the particulate air.

"We're all going to die here," Shawna said from behind a foam gravestone.

"No we're not, we've got enough food and water to last a lifetime," I said.

Melissa, our skinny vegan, said, "It's not food, it's processed. We're totally going to die."

"This is bullshit," Davis said.

"This is retribution," Søren said. Søren was a goth kid, maybe in his early twenties, tubby and morose. That, I remember, was the first time he'd said anything to any of us. With his black lipstick and fishnets, he appeared at home in the wrecked graveyard in which we were arguing out our fate.

"So he can talk," Speck said.

"Retribution for what?" Ron said.

"For building this place. For playing God. For filling it with trinkets in which we've tried to place transcendent meaning."

"What in the world are you talking about?" I said.

"I'm talking about death."

"What's with this philosophical bullshit?" Speck said. He

was the only one who'd elected to not shower in the gardening department and who'd refused to pick himself new clothes. His tie-dye had dulled to the luster of old stained glass, and his ass-length ponytail seeped grease.

"It's your life," Søren said.

"It's stupid," Speck said.

"Exactly."

"I don't have to listen to this," Ron said, walking away.

"We're all here for a reason," Søren said.

"There's no reason. It's totally random," Shawna said. "My mother was going to come, but she tore a ligament in her foot. It could have just as easily been her in here."

"Your mother's accident means you were meant to come."

"There is no meaning," I said, surprised at what had come out of my mouth.

vi. Bottle

Since then, we've organized four more attempts. The store's layout doesn't shift like in a science fiction movie. There are no supernatural forces at play. The place is simply too vast, too confusing, and the longer we stay here the less adept we become at navigating via intuition. The sensory cues human beings normally rely upon are scrambled, subverted by impossible angles, shimmering towers, corridors which run for miles and terminate in foggy manmade moraines.

Sometimes, I don't know why we so desperately want to leave. In our former lives, we were drawn to places like this, as babies to a breast. In the store, the uncontrollable world is broken down and reconstituted as something logical, manageable, meaningful. There is heroism in erecting a citadel like this, in navigating it, in seeking out and finding magnificence in its offerings. Maybe Søren is right—maybe this is a place of death, or, conversely, of life everlasting.

vii. Pills

IN THE morning, I find Davis's body in the pharmacy. He's taken an overdose of sleeping pills. I kneel down and pat his forehead, not knowing what else to do. Through the drive-thru window, I see the doughy face of a man in an SUV. I leave Davis's body and run toward the window waving my arms, but the man stares right through me. He looks at his watch and drives away.

We put together a service for Davis in the ruined graveyard. Shawna looks mad. I ask her why the long face?

"He's a giver-upper. We can't have that here," she says.

"He was unhappy."

"We're all unhappy."

"I'm not actually all that unhappy," Speck says.

"Are you serious?" Ron asks.

"I'm totally serious."

"Have you been raiding the SSRIs again?" I ask.

Speck smiles, a sunlit blankness in his eyes, like light through bathwater.

"Not cool," Ron says.

"What's the big deal?"

"The big deal is that you're not genuinely dealing with your emotions. And also, those pills belong to the store."

"Why should I genuinely deal with my emotions?"

"To find out what's really bothering you," Shawna says.

"I already know what's bothering me. I'm trapped in a place I can't find my way out of, even though it should be easy. All bets are off. People on the outside munch these like they're M&Ms. I think I have a pretty good reason."

"He's right," Søren says. "Why not feel groovy if we're going to be stuck here."

"Did he say 'groovy?'" I ask.

"Are you popping pills too?" Shawna asks.

"What if I am?"

"You're a poser, with your dark clothes and death-talk."

"I'm not a poser," Speck protests. "I'm experimenting with happiness. It may turn out it's not for me."

viii. Radishes

TWO WEEKS go by. A somnolence falls over us. Shawna abandons her diagram. Davis's body starts to stink, so I put it in the walk-in freezer. Speck's eyes are quivering yolks. I tell him to quit with the pills and he says he's over it: happiness isn't all it's cracked up to be.

Ron tells me that he saw Jesus in produce, and I roll my eyes. He says to go look if I don't believe him. I find a bundle of ruby-red radishes on the aisle's buffed floor, conspicuously placed like an offering. In the texture of the vegetables' bright skin I see clouds, sunbeams.

"What's with the radishes?" Søren asks, standing over me.

"They're so beautiful," I say.

"Like the hearts of angels," he says. I look up at him. He has taken to wearing brightly-colored women's clothes, makeup, high heels. He tells me that the SSRIs have helped him become more comfortable with his femininity. I tell him I think this newfound sense of self is great, but that it's too bad it had to be a result of our situation. His overpowering maternal presence releases something in me. I confide in him that I'm losing hope.

"What do the radishes say? Can you read something in their skin?"

"Whatever they're telling me remains obscure."

ix. Ice Cream Sandwich

THE OTHERS become curious about Davis's body. They request to see it. Speck is the first. He comes to me at night, stinking of alcohol, eating an ice cream sandwich. The chocolate is smeared across his lips, lending him a clownish air.

"I need to get closer to death," he says.

"Suit yourself," I say, yanking open the freezer door. I watch him through the condensation on the door's little window. He kneels at Davis's abdomen, puts his hand on the man's cold heart. I think I see him wipe a tear from his eye. When he comes out, there are little icicles hanging from the underside of his nose.

I ask Søren if he'd like to see the body, but he demurs. "In my former life I would have been the first inside the freezer, believe you me. I would have thought it was cool. 'Ooh, I'm gonna see a dead body.' Thanks, but no thanks. I've turned over a new leaf."

x. Frosting

THE FOOD starts to get low. I pretend I don't notice. Shawna starts a new mural in the unisex bathroom, this time using chocolate frosting. The mural doesn't resemble anything in the outer world—it is alien and internal. I stand staring, perplexed. In the patterns she's drawn I think I see muscles, arteries, organs.

"What is it?" I ask.

"It's a map of my inner-space," she says. "It will help me find my way."

"Are you feeling okay?"

"I'm retreating into myself."

"That doesn't sound good," I say.

"It's the only way to combat this place. I'm beginning to see myself for who I am: a body, prone to decay, miraculous rumblings, pulsations, inner secrets. It's like for years I've just been this brain floating in space! Look at my fingers, look at my toes! Why do we put nail polish on our fingernails? Lipstick on our lips? It's not to draw attention but to cover up, to obscure the reality."

"What's the reality?"

"That we're animals. Creatures. That we will one day die."

"Are you on something?"

"Speck had a sheet of blotter acid. He said he was saving it for if he ever got out of here, but he's given up hope."

xi. Beach Chair

I FIND Speck in the far corner of the warehouse, in a beach chair, staring up through the skylight. I look up: a few tissue-paper clouds decorate an aqua patch of sky. I look back at him. Foamy spittle crawls down his chin. He is wearing women's pajamas.

"What the hell?" I say.

"I've seen it."

"What?"

"The end. In all its glory. It shines behind everything. This whole place is like a fortress against its advance. I know now."

"You're tripping."

"Duh."

"We need to keep our heads, otherwise we'll never get out of here."

"I'm already out of here."

xii. Toilet Paper

I LOOK for Shawna in the restroom. The mural has expanded to the floors, the ceiling. It is as if I've walked into a lower intestine. I find Melissa in front of a toilet, with a roll of toilet paper in her hand. She is staring into the water as if divining the future.

"What are you seeing?"

"That's me in there. Part of me," she says. I walk up behind her. She is trembling like a hatchling. I look down into the toilet. A turd turns in the water like a docking boat. "Have you ever just sat and looked at your poop?"

"Not really. Maybe when I was a kid."

"We need to return to that point. Everything else is just illusion. I'm going to get down on my knees and smell it. You can join me if you like."

"No thanks."

"I'll want access to the walk-in later."

"To see Davis?"

"To see Davis. But also to defrost some meat. I've got this uncontrollable urge to eat meat."

xiii. Greeting Card

IT TURNS out Shane has taken acid, too. And so has Ron, who has gone missing. I find Shane weeping in cosmetics. I try to reassure him, but my entreaties are growing dishonest in the face of our circumstance. All evidence points to being stranded here forever. I see Shane growing old. I see me homeschooling him via paperback thrillers and stolen looseleaf. I see the shelves bare, the lights blinking out one after another. I see darkness, products finally drained of meaning, all that was meant to be unfolding without us, the outside world spiraling off into eternity.

"I wasn't here to buy toilet paper," Shane says. I see shame turning in his eyes. I take his hands. His palms are like pieces of cold pizza dough.

"You weren't?"

"I was here to buy my mom a birthday present. I had such high hopes. I was going to get her something real nice. Maybe from the ladies' aisle."

"Let's pick something out together."

"But it's too late. Her birthday was ages ago. And besides, we're stuck here."

"We're going to get out of here. And you're going to give her her gift. And a card. Mothers love cards."

I take Shane to the greeting cards. We stand twirling the

revolving racks in the cold quiet. Mine squeaks like a hungry mouse. I show Shane a few cards and he just shrugs. "This is so pointless."

"What is?"

"Buying stuff. As if it could ever really mean what you need to it mean, or say what you need it to say, or whatever."

"It's what we do. As humans."

"As stupid humans."

"As stupid humans."

"I guess this one," he says, showing me a card with a hokey illustration of a bouquet of pink roses. "She likes pink."

"Okay, follow me."

We arrive at the ladies' aisle. We look at shampoo, hairbrushes, maxi pads. "This stuff is so weird," he says.

"What did your mom like. I mean, what does your mom like?"

"I don't know. Lady stuff."

"How about this?" I ask, holding up a magnifying makeup mirror. "It's got a light and everything. Does she wear makeup?"

"Tons," he says.

"This is perfect then," I say. "And you can get her some makeup to go with it."

We move down he aisle to the makeup. Shawna is there with Melissa. Shawna is sitting with her head in her hands. Melissa is gnawing on frozen chicken nuggets, occasionally staring at them. "What's going on?" Shawna asks.

"Shane wants to get his mother some makeup. For her birthday."

"What color are her eyes?" Melissa asks.

"Blue."

"Well, how about some of this," Shawna asks, handing him

a shiny bottle of eye shadow. "This is what I'd get if I was lucky enough to have blue eyes."

Shane takes the small bottle and turns it over in his fingers. Behind his hair's waterfall I see his own blue eyes, his mother's eyes, alive with tears. A glob of snot droops from his nose and he sucks it back in. His lower lip quivers like a puddle in the wind. Shawna puts her arm around him, and I join her. Melissa rests her head on his shoulder.

"We're going to get you out of here," I say. Shawna raises an eyebrow at me over Shane's little head. I think of Jenni and Deb and all the hurt I've ever felt gathers around me like mourners at a grave.

We will not die here.

xiv. Mower

"How FAST can these things go?" I ask Ron. We are in Lawn & Garden. I run my hand along the mower's fiberglass body. I kneel down and sight down its length like a member of a NASCAR pit crew.

"Thirty, tops," Speck says.

"That's not so fast," Ron says.

"I can mod it," Speck says. "I mean, after I come down from my trip."

"Mod it how?" I ask.

"Easy. Do a pulley swap. The belt might rub the shifter, but I can see what I can salvage from the other mowers. I can get it up to fifty-five, sixty tops. It'll be crazy unstable. Might have to weigh the front down to prevent flipping it."

"Let's do it," I say. "We can hook a cart up to the back and put everyone in."

"This is so dangerous," Melissa says.

"Do you want to eat processed food forever?" I ask.

"No."

"I don't know if I can climb in there with my dress," Søren says.

"I'm scared," Shawna says.

"Beyond fear lies hope," I say.

xv. Sky

I FEEL the engine purr. I rev it. Exhaust blooms, a majestic canopy of optimism. The store's banners are flags snapping me to courage. Cold glory moves through me. Shane's breath is on my neck, his arms around my waist, his nearness like an ocean wave. I love these people: they are my friends. I've learned so much in our time here in the store—what's important, what isn't, what people desire and what they need: so much need. Will this mad flight work? Or will it end in tears and twisted wreckage? Part of what I've been taught by the store is that death is what's most missing from our lives. I put the pedal to the metal. I feel the wind in my teeth. The store's forbidding lights smear into laser beams. We fly. The bristling cornucopia we sail through is not plentitude—it is a magic show promising immortality. There is no pulse here, no blood flows. In the heartbeats of those nearest to me—our little clan—I hear the song of life.

REMINDERS

i.

I AWAKE to blackbirds on the telephone wire strung like jewels across the sky. I walk to the window and one by one their heads turn toward me. Are they harbingers, or just things in the world, dumb and unknowing? A light snow emits from oily clouds. I glance down into the yard. Someone has pulled one of my picnic benches up beneath the window.

Outside, I inspect the bench's surroundings. I kneel and find a scattering of chewed fingernails, a cigarette butt, a candy wrapper. It's the same brand of bar I enjoyed too often as a teen, with the consequence of suffering lifelong dental problems. I turn the wrapper over in my hand, take in its familiar synthetic texture. There is chocolate smudged on the inside, and several small worms wriggle through it.

I notice a wet spot on the cement. I run my finger through it and bring it to my nose. Sticky-sweet, gingery, like soda pop.

In the kitchen, I wash my hands once, twice, three times. I drink my fresh-squeezed juice. I open my pill container and take my aspirin, C60, lithium, and oxaloacetate. I listen to the highway through the window. No one ever visits; the phone seldom rings. The mail is all junk, and the neighbors never say hello.

ii.

THE FOOTSTEPS begin soon after. The wood floors in my house are prone to creaking, and when I step, I hear a mimicry of the sound elsewhere in the house. These echoes occur almost simultaneously with my own steps. If I am downstairs, they occur above; if I am upstairs, I hear them below. There is a mocking quality to these replica steps. I have become the butt of a joke.

Two nights after the footsteps begin, I am standing in the kitchen peering out into the black slate of night. The streetlight casts papery shadows on the lawn. A car passes, throwing bright javelins into the yard. This is when I see him—a man, hunched against the cold, hands thrust in pockets, walking across the lawn around the side of my house. He has a cigarette between his lips, and, via the glow from its lit end, I can make out the barest outlines of his face: pock-marked, doughy, with a pained expression not unlike my own.

I follow him from window to window as he heads to the backyard. I see him sitting on the bench in the shadows, waiting. For a long while, he sits. Eventually, he stubs out his cigarette. Sparks bloom by his feet as if in celebration. The man that looks like me gets up and walks to the house's rear screen door. I stand frozen. I hear the hinges squeak, slam, and then the footsteps that soon blend with my own. I search the house, but he is nowhere to be found.

iii.

I spend an afternoon listening to the ancient healing codes of the Solfeggio Scale. I used to listen to pop, or jazz, but the inherent atonality of most modern music made me ill. This sickness manifested itself as shakes, rigors, cold sweats, pains in my lower back and testicles. Ever since, this has been my daily ritual, a temporary entrance into a cathedral built of celestial timbres. While I sit and listen, I eat my customary kale salad, drink my probiotic cocktail, and sort my vitamins. It is a bitter, gray day, and the dull swatch of the sky through the window serves as a canvas onto which I paint thoughts of eternal youth.

iv.

Signs of the bench-sitter's presence manifest in the house. I find candy wrappers on the living room floor, and empty chip bags in the basement. He has switched on the television—an old tube relic which I seldom watch—and tuned it to a public access station. All night the channel broadcasts quickly edited montages of car accidents. One after another, a concussive succession of twisted metal and fire. The sound of these crashes has been stripped out and replaced with loud guitars and guttural screaming.

My VCR—long out of service and stored in the basement—reappears, hooked to the upstairs television. Inside I found a tape, which contains footage of what appears to be a hospital procedure. Glistening organs, scalpels, and viscera splash across the screen.

I find excrement in unflushed toilets. Cigarettes burning at the lips of sinks. Books taken from shelves and left open, volumes from my angry alienated days. The pages smell of stale smoke. I recall my old habit: singed lungs and tarry fingers. I remember my ex-girlfriend, Jacqueline, her coffee breath, her cat with its dirty litter box.

I call 911, and two bored policemen arrive and tour the house. I show them the cigarette butts, the bench outside, food that has gone missing from the refrigerator.

"You live alone?" one of them says.

"Yes."

"Are you sure?"

"Am I sure I live alone?"

"You've had no visitors you know of."

"Well, this is a visitor, is he not?"

"I'll rephrase: no visitors you've expressly invited inside your domicile?"

"Of course not."

"We'll make a note of this. Fill out a blotter sheet."

"That's it? Have there been other break-ins in the neighborhood?"

"Not that we are aware of."

"Thank you."

"Sir, keep your doors locked."

I TRY to put all thoughts of the visitor out of my mind. I resume my routine: two hours of cardio on the elliptical in the morning, followed by my pill regimen, yoga, and raw juice. I take to wearing my crystal again, although it was receiving snickers at work. I add several more layers of tinfoil to the smart meter in the basement. The user @AngelTom on www.liveforever.com suggested more foil if I was still experiencing ill effects. I'd already moved my Faraday cage up to the second floor, and then the attic. It is a top-of-the-line model, guaranteed to shield me from 99.9 percent of all electrical fields, radio waves, and wireless signals.

At night, safe inside my cage, I dream of satellites tumbling through space. I dream of solar flares, the planet gone black, civilization returned to the Paleolithic. I run through the primeval forests, tossing boulders with my bare hands. I am alive! But then I am awoken by a noise in the house. It is him. I collapse back into fraught dreams of something red, and wet, and malign.

vi.

I CLEAN up after him. I purchase several secondhand ashtrays and empty them regularly. I flush toilets, wash dishes. He takes to sleeping on the sofa in the basement, which I persistently vacuum of crumbs and ashes.

He brings items in off the street—worn hollow doors,

chunks of styrofoam, a piece of a cemetery headstone, old televisions. The TVs pile up, along with various cords and antennae, tape decks, speakers, cassettes.

In the abandoned guest room upstairs, he builds a wall of this outdated equipment. Floor to ceiling the TVs flicker, broadcasting their terrible images: amputees, deformed children, fires, floods, rituals in the neglected woods. I recognize the place—its runs along the underpass behind my house. More tapes piled up, labeled Reminders 1, Reminders 2, Reminders 3, and on and on. This morbid library overtakes the house; soon the tapes are piled everywhere.

I stalk the woods, the crunch of leaves mixed with the scream of tires from the highway. A frost encrusts the ground, but I found one charred, humid place. There are half-melted plastic doll parts here, and what looks like bits of burnt meat. A smashed television sinks into the black earth. Something unspeakable has occurred here, not minutes from my house, and the visitor is its orchestrator.

vii.

THE POLICE make several more visits. They agree to patrol the neighborhood. I escort them out into the woods, where they kick at the charred remains.

"Just some kids messing around."

"Doing what?" I ask.

"Rituals."

I flash back to my teen years. A visit to the bookstore in the mall to purchase a sweet-smelling trade paperback of The Satanic Bible. I think of Rich, my best friend, who was badly burned in fire we'd set together in the woods. I feel the burning smoke in my lungs. The acrid stench returns. The sirens. The news broadcasts.

"Sir?"

"Excuse me, were you saying something?" I say to one of the officers.

"Are you feeling okay, sir?"

"No, I'm not feeling okay. I need this taken care of."

"With no evidence, there's not much we can do."

"There's a burnt baby doll right there! I found feces in my toilet, and it isn't mine."

"This can just be a prank. We've seen it before. It'll die down."

Die down. I focus on the words. I ponder each separately. Die. Down. I see my corpse being lowered into a grave, or tossed, weighted with stones, into the sea.

viii.

I SET up a camera in the woods, a newfangled digital one with a timer. I spend all day online, accumulating specialty surveillance equipment that will allow direct broadcast of the footage to my smartphone.

I crawl into bed, remote-power the camera, and stare through its lens into the tarnished trees. An hour passes, two. I fall asleep. I wake in a cold sweat and open the window. I smell burning leaves, singed plastic. I power up the phone and see a blaze on the screen.

He is there, naked, dancing around the fire. His skin glistens, scars on his chest pulse. He leaves the fire and lunges toward the camera's lens. His face fills my phone's screen. I can't make out his features; they seem to shift with the buzzing grain of the low-light footage. He kneels down and rummages inside a duffel bag. From its black mouth he extracts a plastic baby doll. Taped to its head is a cut-out photo of my face, eyes closed, taken while I was asleep.

I watch as he tosses the me-doll into the fire. I imagine my skin blistering, muscles singeing. My room is hot, I sweat. Cut to a close-up shot of the doll as it melts, tiny eruptions like a time-lapse disease across its melting skin.

The visitor pulls the camera from its stand. I watch a first-person POV shot gliding through the woods. The camera's bright LED light slithers over the grainy underbellies of the trees. From the dark of the wood onto the pocked brightness of the asphalt he crawls, past grim houses, with their bodies in bed, taking in air, breathing out vaporous waste. The streetlights flare like angels in the camera's eye.

Around the corner he floats, down my street, past my neighbor's homes. I pull my sheets to my chin. The frame of the television, for so many years a portal to other worlds, is now a mirror of my own, a bird of prey, an electronic ghost. The wired demon slides across the porch, through the front door, and up the stairs. I watch but I don't believe. I hear no footsteps, only the cold crack of rain. Everything I've kept at bay is brought flooding in with it, a deluge of reminders. At the end of all youthful endeavor, flying in the face of all rituals, he comes. He comes, and he comes, and he comes.

A REASON TO BELIEVE

i.

THERE WAS something deliberate about my wrong turn. I'd taken the same route to and from work for years, but this time an unseen hand was at the wheel. Turning from the familiar thoroughfare, I found myself in a part of town I didn't recognize. Treeless, encased in concrete, stitched together by power lines, it was a hamstrung, utilitarian place. For miles it stretched on, store after store, lifeless and dull. But magic is found in the most unlikely places. Now that I live here, I appreciate the place's wonder. The parking lot is an old friend. And the treasures I have discovered provide more warmth than a million suns.

ii.

I WAS in the midst of a nervous breakdown. Contrary to what I'd seen on television, it wasn't the explosive collapse I was anticipating, but more of a slow glide into the dark. All the possibilities I'd entertained as a young man had slowly closed their doors.

"You don't love us," Chelsea accused, on a silent afternoon.

"It has nothing to do you with you, or the kids. It's me. I feel like something's missing," I said, pointing at my heart, which twitched in anticipation of the brewing argument. I knew she could never comprehend it; I didn't understand it myself.

So many of the things we need exist beyond the margins of the words we have to describe them. A way of putting it was that I was bored with my life. Bored sounds innocuous—something one experiences on a lazy Saturday in wintertime—but boredom can also be a leviathan, casting a shadow as large as the world. To wake in the morning expecting a carbon copy of the previous day's events is equivalent to not waking at all.

iii.

ON MY journey to and from work, I had too much time to think. I drove through the same treeless commercial tract, one long mall alight with logos promising deliverance. It was a place we occasionally came to on weekends to purchase staples for the house: toilet paper, cleaning supplies, garbage bags. Afterwards, we'd flee in search of decent food, or a movie, or some other way to fill the heavy hours before bed.

It was at the intersection of the four gas stations that I took the turn. I felt something calling me. Soon the familiar big boxes and retail behemoths gave way to establishments I didn't recognize. Peculiar B- and C-grade stores huddled together among crumbling sideways and oil-stained lots. On paper it sounds sad, but there was a beauty to it. Patrons with beaming smiles entered and exited doorways with shopping bags bearing catchphrases and trademarks. Children walked hand-in-hand with their parents, licking ice cream cones. Old wooden telephone poles bore armies of rusted staples, the scars of a thousand flyers come and gone.

I turned into one of the crowded lots and parked my car. I sat watching people come and go, clutching their spoils. I was already thirty minutes late to work, but I didn't care. I pulled my wallet from my pocket and fingered my credit card. I could taste it: something here would take the pain away.

iv.

BEFORE MY daughter was born, I used to think the human lust for things was something that advertising nurtured in us. We were born free of all worldly wants beside those of sustenance, warmth, our mother's touch. Soon, the bright objects of childhood were thrust into view—on television, on the shelves of toy stores, or at other, luckier children's homes. This exposure drew attention from the world of grass and earthworms to the realm of brightly molded plastic. This shift seemed to be an ineluctable one.

But as I watched my little one grow, I came to realize that the desire for objects was inborn. What could it be that the developing mind found in lifeless things? What anxieties did their possession assuage? Dolls, tiny cars, kitchen utensils, tarnished pennies, chopsticks, plastic straws, spoons, balls, spray bottles, trowels, cardboard boxes…

Occasionally, under the heavenly lights of the local department store, watching my daughter's eyes sparkle at the sight of a dress, or a pair of shoes, or a new doll, a sorrow would overtake me. Not even five years into life, and already a flight into dead material hands. This desire struck me as animal its stupidity, yet animals have no need for malls, factories, shoe outlets.

But then the glossy footpath would lead us into the Men's Department, and my heart would thump at the thought of just one tiny purchase: a new tie, a watch, a fountain pen. In that moment, one of these objects became more important to me than my family. To take it home in its satiny bag, to hold it in my arms like a newborn, to wake in the middle of the night remembering its nearness—these things were more comforting than any warmth another person could supply. I'd be ashamed at this prospect, but also thrilled. Humans live and die, relationships wither, children grow old. But the stores were eternally replenished.

v.

I EXITED the car and stretched. The noonday sun beat down. Kids laughed; music played. I approached a concrete esplanade which separated the shops from the lot. I peered down the row of storefronts. I was two hours late for work but I didn't mind. My phone would ring on my dashboard with no one to hear.

A young woman strode past me. In her arms, she was holding some gleaming thing that shone with an inner light. She cradled it; her face spread into a smile like a warm bath. I could smell it on her, the desperation evaporating like dew, replaced by sunlight and blue sky. I studied the thing she held, but the closer I looked, the more diffuse it became. It shifted and rippled at her breast like an atomic particle.

I left her and walked, gazing through the windows. Here there were no shoes, no dresses, no vacuum cleaners, no painkillers. Everything bristled with newness. The signs led me from place to place: SALE, 50% OFF, LIMITED TIME ONLY, BUY 2 GET 1 FREE, SHOP N' SAVE!

I stopped and stretched. An ethereal silence moved across the lot. I noticed none of the cars were leaving, and none were entering. Shoppers returned to their vehicles, bags in tow, and sat inside, gazing at their items. Others left their vehicles, empty packages in their hands, and were drifting silently around to the rear of the building.

vi.

I FOLLOWED a woman who stepped from her Range Rover. Her cheeks were sooty with mascara, as if she'd been crying. She trudged, empty box in hand, around the corner where the shops terminated in a blind alley. I kept my distance. Bits of trash littered the neglected alleyway's curbs. Unused and rusty Dumpsters leaned at resigned angles. I heard the doleful cry of a train's whistle. I didn't like it here, but resisted the urge to turn back.

The woman rounded the corner and disappeared from view. I hesitated by a sewer grate, fiddling with my phone. Within a few moments, the woman returned, no longer holding her box. She approached me without a look, rifling through her purse and withdrawing a glossy credit card. She appeared more hopeful than before; there was a modest brightening in her eyes, a quickening in her step. I felt an immense attraction to this woman, as if I were a peg that would fit into a hole in her heart. She ignored me and went about her way.

From around the corner, at the back of the row of stores where the woman had vanished, came the mechanical lurch of a garbage truck. The sound—monstrous, violent—struck a nerve. I fled the alley and returned to the bright facade of storefronts.

I picked a shop and stepped inside. A bell rang, and a young woman with strawberry hair looked up from behind her register. "Please let me know if I can help you find what you're looking for," she said.

I roamed the aisles. Gentle music wafted. Time melted like ice cream in the sun. A woman who was stocking shelves said to me: "Please let me know if I can help you find what you're looking for." I looked closely at her face. She resembled the woman at the front who'd greeted me when I came in; perhaps they were twins.

"I don't know," I said.

"Please don't hesitate to ask," she sang, and returned to carefully restocking a shelf with small gleaming boxes. The items' packaging was minimally designed, attractive in a modern, sustainable way: recycled materials, warm organic inks, sophisticated typefaces. I leaned in closer and plucked one of the boxes from the shelf. The dimensions seemed perfectly formulated to fit in my hands.

"What do we have here?" I said under my breath. The woman continued to restock the shelves, paying me no attention. The brand name of the product was A Reason to Believe™. The logo was clean and modern, tinted a pleasant grass green, and featured a pictograph of a joyful, smiling person. The box read in bold, blue text: NOW WITH 20% MORE!

I flipped the object over, noticing its feathery weight; it couldn't be a piece of electronic equipment. I shook it and heard nothing. I turned it over again in my hands, scanning the package. There was very little additional information. I imagined myself exiting the store empty-handed and my mood took a swift dive.

"How much is this one?" I asked.

"$149.99," she said.

"Are any of these on sale?"

"That is the sale price."

"What is it, anyway?"

"It's a reason to believe," she answered.

"Huh. I think I'll take this one," I said.

"Come around to the register," she barked, perhaps irritated that I had interrupted her progress restocking the shelves. I followed her through the aisles. The scent of fabric softener brought me back to brighter days. I thought of my mother, and how many hours she spent in the laundry room. I recalled sugary cereal and Saturday-morning cartoons. There was a time when things were promising for me. What was I doing here, away from my job, my family, my humdrum life?

At the register, the woman punched in the item code and spun the small digital checkout screen toward me. I inserted my card and signed my name with my finger.

"Receipt?" she asked.

"I don't think I'll need one," I replied.

"Nobody's ever returned one of these," she said, looking up at the television that hung in the high corner. A news anchor said, "It remains an active shooter situation. All nearby schools and business are in lockdown, and we urge all residents to remain safely indoors."

Outside, I scurried to my car. The sun was setting. The lot was still full, with people coming and going from their cars, vanishing down the alley, and returning empty-handed.

I opened the passenger-side door and sat down—I had an odd compulsion to sit there instead of the driver's seat. For a long minute I sat with the box in my lap. The anticipation was delicious, like a crisp, freshly picked apple raised to my lips. I looked at my phone and saw 17 missed calls, some from the office, some from home. I rolled down the window and inhaled. The odor of parking lots everywhere greeted me: asphalt, motor oil, rainwater, the lack of all things organic. I began to pry at one of the box's expertly machined cardboard flaps when my phone rang. It was Chelsea.

viii.

I reached for the phone, listened to it ring a second, third, fourth time. Already I felt my wife receding from me. My career as a father and husband was a noble yet failed effort.

What had gone wrong? It was not two years into our marriage when, one morning over breakfast, I was assaulted by the realization that my life was a source of perennial dissatisfaction. That each thing gained was merely a signpost pointing to another desire, each accomplishment a reminder not of fullness but of lack. This frustration prevented me from receiving and expressing love, both toward my wife and my child. Why? Three different therapists had failed to offer an explanation, or, in the language of therapy, failed at helping me find a reason inside myself.

The only way I knew how to explain was with the words of a child: I wanted what I wanted when I wanted it. And if thwarted, I'd lash out at whoever was nearest, most of the time my wife and daughter. Chelsea, who had long ago mastered the art of beatitude, could forego all immediate pleasures in lieu of providing for us. She had grown up; I'd remained a child. And instead of admiring this in her, I'd come to resent it, and to feel ashamed for doing so. Eventually, shame won, as it is wont to do in a life without tether to larger principles.

ix.

So, WITH great satisfaction, I didn't answer my phone. The pain this caused felt good, like digging a fingernail into a mosquito bite. It was something I could do again and again, and feel alive doing, unlike the life I'd been leading up until now. Denial gave me control.

With this I tore into the package. I sensed the supple cardboard bend beneath my dumb fingers. It felt good to destroy what had been designed to appear everlasting. The odors of fine paper and industrial ink greeted my nostrils. One flap, two flaps, three. Just the last remained. An excitement not dissimilar to sexual arousal flooded my belly and gripped my hips.

I lifted the flap.

Nothing.

A lead bolt of anger shot through me. How could they do this? Surely this must be a mistake. I reached inside, felt the smooth fleshy insides of the box, turned it upside-down, held it up to my face and nearly cried into its barren depths.

And then I was reminded of how good it felt, before I discovered that emptiness. How the expectation had fingered a sexual part of me, arousing something ancient and all-encompassing.

I reached inside again, as a child engages in magical thinking. There was a time in life when something could come from nothing, when a void could give birth to something wanted, something needed.

And then I felt it.

A tiny slip of paper.

I pulled it up into the car's fading light. A piece of heavy, luscious card stock, with embossed green type that read: PLEASE RECYCLE THIS PACKAGE.

Accompanying the words was a small, elegantly designed diagram: the strip mall's lot, as seen from overhead, and my car, highlighted in viridescent ink, with a curvaceous dotted line proceeding from the passenger-side door, around the corner, down the alleyway, and to the back of the building.

x.

I LEFT the car. There were more of us now, holding our empty boxes, some weeping, others resigned, still others in states of confused glee. We passed into the alley, walked among the Dumpsters, stretched our steps through the diffident puddles and sad detritus.

Around the corner we went, single file. There, between the mall's rear cinderblock wall and the railroad tracks, towered a shining mountain of empty boxes. Each of us took his or her turn, tossing our packages into the trembling pile.

"Clear the way," I heard someone shout. I turned to see two men, wearing uniforms emblazoned with A Reason to Believe logos, carrying the body of an old woman. "We've got another one to dispose of here, please step aside."

"Where are they taking her?" I asked a woman who stood behind me in line.

"To the beyond. It's where they put us when we're done."

"Done doing what?"

"Done doing this," she said, and tossed her box into the pile and, prying her credit card from her wallet, walked off down the alleyway into the falling night.

xi.

EVERY MORNING, I wake and make my purchase. I hobble back to the car and sit awash in the beautiful anticipation. I've learned to control the trembling, the soft waves that pass through me. It's become a form of sex, but one free of the anxiety that arises from another person's needs. It is only me with my expectation, fine-tuned into a kind of personal pornography. There is no way to describe this beauty other than to say that it is what I've always wanted: to desire a thing that truly never arrives. The deflation is perhaps the most magnificent part, because it announces that I can do it again. I walk with the others, throw my box in the pile, come back out into the world and do it again, and again, and again.

Eventually, my phone stops ringing. The battery dies. I toss it in one of the Dumpsters, where most of us have discarded things that remind us of what we've given up. When my money runs out, I'll get a job in the store, stocking shelves. This way I can keep up with the latest versions, the best sales. The television will bring news of wars, violence in the streets, pandemics, melting glaciers. Eventually we will conspire to unbolt it from its mooring and toss it away with the rest of the objects we no longer need.

Sleep comes easy. I just think about the next day's beautiful thing, in its utter lack, and how, finally, the emptiness in me has met its match. One day, they'll haul me to the beyond, discarded like all things and returned to the dark from which I came.

WINDOWS

i.

FOR TWO strangled months after Melanie died, Jan and I managed to hold on. We hoped we'd be the exception to the rule that marriages never survive the death of a child. But our love had never been strong enough to withstand that kind of storm. For years the cracks had been gathering, hairline fractures I refused to see, things I said or did that belonged to some other person who remained hidden from view.

ii.

WE SOLD the house and Jan moved to a condo near her parents, about two hours away. I rented a dim apartment on the far side of town, far enough away from the places we had known—the sidewalks where Melanie first learned to ride a bike, her school, the streets where Jan and I would walk in the evenings among the complaints of crickets and sprinklers.

Before the funeral I had put my window-cleaning business, Clear as a Bell, on hiatus. Soon after, eager to resume a normal life, I began advertising again. A week to the day after running my first ad—on what would have been my daughter's seventh birthday—I received a voicemail from a new customer who identified herself as Melanie. When I hung up the phone I stood before the old bay window of the house and, for the first time since my little girl's passing, cried for what I'd lost.

iii.

UP TO that point I hadn't grieved properly. I realize this now. To grieve was to give in to the suspicion that my life had been destined for tragedy. Instead, I blinded myself to it all: the funeral, the visits and cards, the thoughts and prayers. Grief repressed returned at night wearing a mask of anxiety. It stalked my bedsheets, my pillow. Everything comfortable became murder and poison and tumors waiting to be found. But soon I became adept at occluding it. I busied myself with mundane things. I fantasized, hid my feelings. And for a time, it felt good.

iv.

MELANIE LIVED in a meager brick ranch on a dead-end street. It was the last house before the block ended in a rusty guardrail, beyond which huddled a dismal patch of woods. If I listened closely, I could hear the faint asthmatic breath of the interstate.

I walked up the path and did what was habitual when approaching a dwelling of any sort—I took stock of the windows. Bay windows? Casements? Transoms? One story or two? Melanie's house seemed, at first glance, to have no windows at all. Typical of mid-century ranches, the ones I did find were more like the embrasures of a medieval castle than anything designed to let light in. These somnolent eyes sat high up, behind the shrubbery, crammed like afterthoughts under the house's aggrieved awnings.

The place produced an uneasy feeling in me. At first, I couldn't locate the source. And then it came to me—the house closely resembled my childhood home. My father, himself a window cleaner who'd taught me the trade, had purchased the house in the early '70s after we moved to the suburbs from the city.

I remembered my first lesson, my father up on his ladder, squeegee in hand and a bucket of sudsy water dangling from his belt. Dad taught me that there was no better way to transform a space than to clean its windows. "Over time, a film of dust and grime coats the window, little by little, until the light dims," he'd say in his customary measured tone. "You may not even be aware of it, like a cataract that forms over the eye."

Then he'd lapse into concentrated silence. The only sounds would be the splash and drip as he brought the squeegee up to the window's pane. One, two, three deft strokes, starting at the top and working his way down. There is nothing more satisfying, I would come to learn, than cleaning a window. Soon the water grows gray and the window shines. The squeegee lets out a crisp squeak, and you move on.

I stood on Melanie's lawn and let these memories flood me. Jan often accused me of sanitizing the past. She disliked how I whitewashed childhood's darker realities. But I chose to look at the bright side. Of all the things Dad taught me, the most important lesson was that stains were never permanent.

v.

WAS MY father good to me? Was I a good father? These are the questions that scrape at the edges of my sleep at night, or during bright days when I'm up on my ladder, ensconced in work. I can't help but think labor is a way of avoiding introspection, and perhaps this is why men excel at their occupations.

Mostly what comes back to me are those last months of Melanie's life. I learned many lessons during her illness, one of which is that despair comes in many guises: as a stormy blast that knocks you off your feet, or as quiet pangs in the dead of night, or in a bereaved mother's voice when she screams at you to leave the room where you once conceived a life together in love and hope.

But what of Melanie? What was she feeling? The inner life of a child is a book written in a foreign language. Or better yet, no language at all. There is so much they don't yet have words for. As they grow—if they have the chance—they learn to translate feeling into words, experience into description. But there are things, I know now, that can never be described.

vi.

I RANG Melanie's bell. At first, I thought I heard a groan or howl, but it was some other noise—a chair skidding across a floor, or maybe a television. After several long moments, the front door creaked and a woman's face materialized like a splotch in the dark.

"Who is it?" she asked.

"Clear as a Bell?" I sang.

"Was it today?"

"That's what you said on the message," I said, checking my clipboard. Somewhere beyond the row of houses, I could hear children playing. Behind the chaos of laughter, I thought I heard crying.

"It looks like rain," she said, craning to look past me at the empty street.

"It does?" I said, looking up toward the sky. A dark thunderhead loomed where moments ago there was blue sky.

"You should come in," she said.

I found myself hunched in a living room lined with yellowing shag carpet. An armchair sagged in front of an old television.

"Forgive me," Melanie said, holding her forehead. "My thoughts have been cloudy."

"Care to show me the windows you'd like cleaned?" I asked.

For a few moments, she stared through me. The house was small, the ceilings low. As I stood in the feeble light, the walls closed in. The suburban boom of the postwar era was remembered as one of emancipation, but the houses it left behind felt like prisons to me. Their dim, stuffy interiors struck me as places where dreams went to die.

"This isn't going to be like your normal job," Melanie said.

"How do you mean?" I asked.

"I found a new room in the house. One that wasn't there before."

"Excuse me?" I heard myself say. The sun threw three sharp beams through the door's staggered windows onto her face.

In this sudden light, I realized Melanie was older than my first impression. I turned, and through the door's tiny panes I could see the sun sliding behind the roofs. Windows were growing purple with twilight. Had that much time passed?

vii.

I will stop here and explain. It is easy for a grieving man to be dishonest. In telling his story, he seeks to rescue what's left of the wreckage of life and cast it in a more utopian light. The death of a child is the figurative death of a parent, a severing of a life from its future purpose. Sometimes it is necessary to resuscitate the past by artificial means. So, there are things I tell myself about Melanie's abbreviated life that aren't entirely true. But every day I grow more honest with myself. But often what shines through is darkness. I may show you why as it becomes clearer.

viii.

I followed Melanie down a cramped corridor whose walls were crammed with bric-à-brac. At the end of the hall hung a thrift shop painting of a pink balloon in a worn wicker frame. Melanie stopped to admire it. The image, with its childish brushstrokes, struck an atonal chord in me. It was still reverberating as Melanie turned to a closed door and said, "Here it is."

"This is the room?"

"Go on, open it."

I turned the knob. The door swung open to reveal a child's bedroom. I stepped in and Melanie followed. The wood floor sighed underfoot. The room was featureless except for a tiny bed and a small closet with a louvered door. A single slender window graced the far corner where the north- and northeast-facing walls joined.

"That's the window?"

"If this room's going to be here, it should be cleaned."

I stepped up to the window. Dust and cobwebs caked its panes. I ran a finger through the grime and it barely relented; a few solemn motes threw themselves into the air. I could hear Melanie wheezing, and the click of her throat as she swallowed, and the blood in my veins.

I turned to her, and she said, "My, you're as pale as a ghost."

ix.

IT'S HARD to think when you live alone. This is something that people with families rarely experience. To be alone, in empty rooms, is to inhabit yourself. And this forces you to accept an important truth: the things that are closest to us are the things we push furthest away, especially on silent afternoons when the hours creep like mold across our thoughts.

On one of my first nights in the apartment, I sat alone at the dining table, eating a frozen dinner. It was one of those late spring evenings, where it seemed like the day would never end. I recalled this feeling from childhood—the anticipation of summer, the expectation that all would be well. A family passed the window. A mother, a father, and a young girl. The girl was clutching the string of a pink balloon.

And it came to me, but not without resistance: a day at the zoo with Melanie. It was early in her illness; my anxiety was acute, but I was keeping it bottled. I went through the motions—the animals in cages, the ice cream stand, the gift shop at the end of a long day. Jan kept sending me scornful looks. We knew our days with Melanie were numbered. Jan took this information like a benediction; I was on the verge of collapse.

I said no to the gift shop; Melanie begged and cried. Her mother relented and took her inside. Soon they emerged with Melanie clutching the string of a shiny pink balloon. On the way back to the car, Melanie did or said something that set me off—I no longer remember what it was. It was a child's natural defiance, a way to seize control of a life that was passing her by.

"You're doing it again," Jan said.

"What am I doing?"

"You're scaring her. She doesn't need this."

My anger grew. Jan told me to calm down. A screaming fight ensued. I grabbed Melanie's balloon and, between my shaking hands, squeezed it until it popped, the sound ringing out like cannon fire across the sky.

x.

MELANIE AND I stepped outside into the twilight. I listened to my feet crunch on the grass. Melanie trod so lightly as to be silent. For a moment, I had the impression that she had no feet. She led me around the side of the house where we again encountered the spectral window. It sat low down in a bed of vines. This was the peculiar trick that houses of this sort played— their putative simplicity hid a troubling elasticity of form.

Melanie stared at the window. I said nothing other than, "Just this window cleaned, or all the others?"

"Only this one."

xi.

I ARRANGED with Melanie to come back the following day to begin the job. She said that she'd be out in the morning, "paying visits," but that I could start on the outside and she'd be back before long. I ate dinner in front of the television, desperate to clear my mind. It felt good to sink into the lunatic rhythms of sitcoms, game shows, the ironic mirth. I used to think down on people who watched too much TV, but an escape from the terrible freedom of life seemed, at last, like the only option left.

xii.

I PULLED the pickup into Melanie's driveway and unloaded my equipment. It was a colorless, shining day. The sun's warmth had an odor to it, one that I associated with public pools and tennis courts. A neighbor's wind chime tinkled.

I forgot to tell Melanie that I'd need access to warm water, so I drew some from a faucet I found in the yard and set the bucket out in the sun to warm while I toured the exterior. Like the other houses in the neighborhood, Melanie's wanted to conceal itself behind its thick shrubbery. It only revealed itself in snatches: a swatch of siding here, a patch of brick there, a slight stretch of sandstone that ran for a few feet and was finally swallowed by starved shadows.

How could I have not seen it before? The house more closely resembled ours—my and Jan's—than it did my childhood home. I stood in the gritty light and imagined myself coming home from work, jangling my keys, Melanie running out to meet me, smile ablaze. The memory was indistinguishable from fantasy. Before becoming a father, I daydreamed of scenes like this, cobbled together from movies and television. If Melanie was there to greet me when I returned home, was it truly with a smile? Had she ever run into my arms at all, or did I fabricate these scenes to paper over something else? Perhaps this was what memory was: an inoculation against time's ability to destroy.

After the water had warmed, I started on the window. Dad's hands guided me. Like all tasks that required artful coordination, some days were on, others were off. Today was an off day; the squeegee skipped and stuttered across the panes, spreading grime. The water cooled quickly. The buckle I used to latch the bucket to my belt unsnapped itself and sent my water spiraling into the bushes.

From atop my ladder, I watched Melanie's car inch up the block and settle into place in the driveway. She pulled herself out of the seat and I was stunned by what I saw: a black scowl stretched across her face like a Halloween mask. Before I was aware of her crossing the lawn, she was at the base of the ladder.

"How dare you!" she hissed through her yellow teeth.

"Excuse me?"

And with that she stalked toward the front door, and was swallowed into the house's black mouth.

I KNOCKED. No answer. A skein of clouds spread across the sun. I pushed the door open. The furniture was gone; a veil of dust blanketed the floor. The house's light—already feeble—died. Thunder cracked, and it began to rain. The shag carpets swallowed my feet like wet snow. I collapsed to my hands and knees.

I could hear Melanie running somewhere else in the house, too fast for the feet of an old woman. On all fours, a dog, I followed—through corridors, up and down stairs. Eventually they led me down the hall and into the room.

Upon the white sheets of the small bed lay the body of my dead child. I rubbed at my eyes. At last, here was a stain I couldn't erase. I crawled to the bed and put my arms around her, but it was too late to love as I should have. To the child's bloodless wrist was tied the burst pink balloon, tattered and adrift in the forever-dying light. The balloon's string went up into the beleaguered air, where it terminated in a point of enduring regret.

VOID DOLLS 1979

i.

MAMA'S VOICE came screeching out of the dark, halfway between a scream and a cry. I could have tossed back the covers and gone to see, but I remained frozen. I thought of the alien abduction book I was reading, about how the tiny men would come through the walls at night and paralyze people and take them away into the sky. Maybe, at last, it was happening to me.

Pretending to be asleep, I listened to the squawk of police radios, grim voices, heavy footsteps that weren't our own. And worst of all—Mama's moans and sobs, the sound of which I've carried with me all my life. They come back to me at night, as an old man. Life, I've learned, is full of those sounds.

ii.

IN THE morning, I played dumb. Mama, eyes swollen with tears, slipped into my room. She sat at the edge of my bed and explained that Dad was gone. I was still dreaming, aboard the alien ship, and maybe Mama was too. She ran her hand through my hair and looked out the window at the old oak tree's fingers. I don't remember what else she said; the words didn't carry the weight, which was carried more by her eyes than her mouth.

That unnameable pressure fell on my chest and has never left. Our lives would never be the same.

Then I remembered it was Saturday morning, and we had made plans as a family to go to the circus. "Does this mean we're not going?" I asked, and Mama cried some more.

iii.

School ended a week later, and Mama said she was taking me to her friend Sally's house. I'd only met Sally once, when I was a baby. She lived a few hours away, by the shore, with her two daughters, Hope and Dawn. She said that she couldn't take care of me in the state she was in, and that Sally had offered to help.

"But I can help," I said. Mama explained that she needed to be alone right now. Funeral arrangements needed to be made, the pieces needed to be picked up. I looked at the floor by her feet in the bedroom where Dad had his heart attack and said, "What pieces?"

iv.

We drove through neighborhoods I didn't recognize. The houses got smaller and fewer. Mama smoked, and I listened to tapes on my headphones. I stared out the window, and when I didn't want to look out the window, I looked at the ashtray, which was overflowing. Once, I dared to glance at the rearview mirror where I caught Mama's eyes. They told me that Dad's death had put a hole between us that could never be filled. Mama always told me that I looked so much like him, so all I did was remind her of what she'd lost.

I was convinced she was going to abandon me at Sally's. She'd start a new life, meet a new Dad, have a new son, and live on pretending that there wasn't a hole where Dad and I used to be.

v.

SALLY'S HOUSE was near the ocean, though you couldn't see the water, only feel it. Seagulls drew scribbles in the sky. The pastel houses' paint had been blasted away by wind and sun. Rickety fences collapsed among the small dunes like broken bones. There weren't any sidewalks.

From up on Sally's porch, as Mama rang the bell, I looked behind us. Across the street was an empty lot, one side of which was bordered by a rotting wooden fence. The place was wild, the grass taller than elsewhere. I could make out a few bits of garbage, old tires, broken bottles, but not much else. Something about that place reminded me of the night Dad died.

Sally answered the door and she and Mama hugged. Sally was a bony woman with short brushy hair and papery creases around her mouth. She looked more like a man than a lady. Behind her, in the dim foyer, her two golden-haired daughters peeked out. One looked older than me, the other younger.

"Don't be shy," Mama said, and nudged me inside. The house smelled like the beach—suntan oil and saltwater and sand. Sally had crammed the walls with seaside things—starfish, fishing nets, paintings of sailboats. We were all stranded at sea.

"Why don't you go play?" Sally said, shooing us away. The older girl, Dawn, said, "I don't want to play with him," and the younger girl, Hope, stared at me with her thumb in her mouth.

Sally pulled Dawn aside and whispered something in her ear. Mama paced and smoked and I thought I heard her say, "Better get used to it."

Dawn, cheeks aflame, said, "Come on," to me, and the three of us went downstairs to the den. As we went down, I could hear Mama crying.

vi.

THE DEN was dingy and smelled like rain. There was one tiny window shaped like a porthole, too high to see through. The floor was covered with a shag carpet that my feet melted into as if it were quicksand. All the girls' stuff was strewn about: dolls and dollhouses and little toy strollers and fake plastic babies. I picked up one of the toy babies' bottles. Inside was a shriveled see-through bag filled with something like milk, but bluer and waterier.

"It's poison," Dawn said.

"That dumb Void Baby drank it and died," Hope said, pointing to a naked baby doll face-down in the corner. One of its legs was missing.

"But it was too late, anyway."

"Void Baby?" I said.

"It had already started to change."

"Change how?" I asked.

Hope was looking sideways at me. Her hair was an abandoned bird's nest. She said, "He went into the hole and wasn't the same anymore. Nothing that goes in comes out the same."

"If you're good, we'll show you," Dawn said.

"Show me what?"

"The Void," she said, putting a finger up to her lips and letting out a dramatic shush.

"Wanna watch us play a video game? It's your initiation," Hope said. "You can't see the Void until you've been initiated."

"I guess," I said.

The girls had a game system I'd never seen before, called Archon II. The console had two wooden paddles with gold wheels on them that you used to control your character. They only had one game named Void Quest. In the game, your character was a square which you moved around a maze looking for keys to unlock doors. The doors seemed to open onto only more rooms, harder mazes, more locked doors.

"What's the point?" I asked.

"There's no point," Hope said.

"You supposedly have to find the treasure before the time runs out," Dawn said.

"What happens if it runs out?" I said.

"The Devourer comes and kills you," Hope explained.

"But we gave up looking for the treasure. It's impossible to find," Dawn said.

"What are you looking for then?" I asked.

"The Dead Spot," Dawn said.

"She calls it the Dead Spot, but it's a nothing spot, really," Hope said.

"It's a part of the game that's broken. It's hidden near a wall somewhere."

"What happens if you find the spot?" I asked.

"Nobody knows."

"That doesn't sound fun," I said.

For a while I watched Hope guide her small square through the dumb gray labyrinth. The game seemed unfinished, as if the game's designer had given up halfway through the creation of his game.

vii.

I DON'T remember how long I sat watching Dawn play. At some point heard Mama's car start up and drive away. The evening sun dribbled through the tiny window. I could smell Sally's cigarette smoke and hear a television elsewhere in the house. A TV newswoman said, "The killer, who is still at large, is thought to be responsible for thirty-four brutal attacks the area, fourteen of them fatal."

I was hungry.

"It's time to see the Void Dolls," Dawn said, throwing down the game controller and turning off the TV.

"What?" I said.

"The Void Dolls. Don't you want to see them?" Hope asked.

"Gather your babies," Dawn said. Each of the girls picked up one of the baby dolls. I fished one out of a bent stroller in the corner. One of its eyes was stuck closed. It had scuff marks on its head as if the girls had beaten it against a brick wall.

"Your baby looks like it's struggling to live," Hope said. "It's a damned shame."

I followed the girls through a door that led to the house's backyard. It was getting dark; a pink glow poisoned the horizon. Dawn saw me looking into the sky and said, "It's World War Three. That's the fallout from the nuclear bombs."

I followed them across the cracked street, around potholes

the size of craters. At the bottom of one, I saw a baby doll face-
down in gray water. The wreckage of a toy carriage lay upended
near the crumbling curb.

THE LOT was wilder than it had appeared from the porch. Shards
of broken glass and cigarette butts littered the sandy ground.
We went single-file through a narrow path of weeds. I could
smell burnt rubber and gasoline as we pushed into the tall
grass. The sunlight turned a tarnished gold and splashed itself
across the fence that bordered the lot. Soon it would leave us.

"You can't tell anyone about what we are about to show you,"
Hope said, turning back to me. "Otherwise, we'll throw you in."

"In where?"

"Into the Void, you dummy."

We trudged on. It seemed we'd been walking much farther
than was possible, given the size of the lot. We passed a car
door without its car, smashed and covered in graffiti. The sun
fell behind the houses. The ocean grew louder. Gulls screamed
overhead. Clouds raced in, their bellies on fire. My stomach
grumbled.

The girls led me to a small concrete building with crumbling
walls. There was a broken stairway that led into a tiny door in
its side.

"Go in," Hope commanded.

I crept up to the opening and peered inside. I could see an
old tire, broken glass, chunks of concrete, and something else
I couldn't make out.

"Don't be chicken," Dawn said.

I stepped inside. In the room's corner leaned a rickety toy crib. I stepped over the garbage and looked down inside.

There were things there on the mattress—what looked like a pile of baby dolls—but the more I looked at them, the less sense they made. I couldn't tell if it was because I was hungry, or because it was dark, but the harder I stared at the tangle of plastic limbs, the weirder they seemed, as if they had been dissected and reassembled in impossible ways. Feeling sick, I stumbled out of the building into the escaping light.

"Did you seem them?" Hope asked.

"What did you do to them?" I said.

"We put them in the Void. And when they came out, they didn't make sense no more."

ix.

We walked on. I thought about the Void Dolls. Something terrible had happened to them, something I didn't have words for. I thought about my life, and how lately it seemed to be just as tangled and impossible to understand as the doll-things I'd seen in the crib.

We emerged from the grass into a small clearing. Dawn took off her clothes. Hope did the same. "What are you doing?" I asked, my cheeks hot with shame.

"You can't go near it with clothes on, stupid," Hope said.

"Why not?"

"Because it won't recognize you."

"I don't want to take my clothes off."

"Then you'll have to wait here."

I sat alone as the girls slipped into the grass. At first, I heard their footsteps, and then only the hiss of the ocean. I thought of Dad, of a trip we once all took together to a seaside town. It was like this one, only brighter, livelier. We stayed in an old inn that smelled of greasy bacon and stale coffee. We took walks to the shore where there was an amusement park. I rode the carousel while dad took pictures. Halfway through our last day, Dad fell into one of his bad moods. While I was off playing games, I could hear Mama arguing with him. I wanted to stay in the park forever. Soon night came, and it was time to go home.

On our way back, we passed a magic shop, and I begged to go inside. Dad said no, but Mama grabbed my hand and led me through the doors. She bought me a deck of magic cards. Tearing into the package, I learned that the deck wasn't really magic. It was just a cheap trick. They cut the cards so that one side of each was a slight bit wider than its opposite. If you asked a member of your audience to pick a card, and placed it back reversed, you could easily swipe it out of the deck. The slight thrill that came with learning the trick turned into disappointment. There wasn't any magic, only illusion, and magic and illusion weren't the same.

x.

THE GIRLS were gone forever. I thought Sally would call for us, but she didn't. Eventually, I heard the tiny crunch of footsteps. Hope came out of the grass with a weird look on her face, hugging her naked chest. She didn't seem like a little girl anymore.

"What happened?" I asked.

"Dawn went inside. We were just supposed to put a doll in. Like all the times before."

"Where is she?"

"She won't come. Can you help me get her?"

I followed her through the grass; its teeth bit at my arms. I could barely make out Hope's ghostly body ahead; it became part of the shadows. I wondered what it would be like to touch her skin, how it would feel to kiss her lips. It seemed just as senseless as what I'd seen in the crib, something I had no way of describing to myself.

We came to a rubbly clearing. The remnants of some ruined structure poked through the ground. It reminded me of an archeologist's dig I'd seen on TV. The wooden fence stretched off as far as the eye could see.

Hope pointed. Past the ruins, near the fence, was an enormous hole in the ground. It seemed to swallow all light. A few of the girls' dolls littered its murky lip. Dawn sat at the hole's mouth, hugging her knees.

"I'm scared," I said.

"Mama's going to be angry," Hope said.

I walked over to Dawn. She heard me, but didn't look up, only stared down into the cavity at her feet.

"Come on, we have to go," I said.

"It's all just so stupid," Dawn said.

"What is?"

"Everything."

"Ask her what she saw," Hope demanded.

"I saw nothing," Dawn said. I looked at her black hair crawling over her shoulders. Pressed between her knees and arms I could make out the fleshy skin of her breasts.

"We have to go or we'll be in trouble," I said.

"Mama doesn't care," Dawn said.

Behind me, I heard Hope crying. "Tell her not to say it," Hope pleaded trough her snotty sobs.

"She cares," I said, even though nobody seemed to care about us.

"All these kid games, they're stupid," Dawn said.

"No, they're not!" Hope said.

"It's different now," Dawn said.

"What's wrong with her?" Hope pleaded, sniffling. "What's different?"

"Everything."

xi.

In the morning, Sally woke me to say she was leaving for work. Breakfast was on the table; lunch was in the refrigerator. She stank of cigarettes, which reminded me of mom. She didn't smile, just rattled off a few more instructions and left.

I fell back asleep and was woken by a thumping sound from the yard. I stood up on the bed and pried the blinds apart. Dawn was outside tossing toys into a garbage can. Hope was dumping coloring books into a bonfire. They were both naked. Sparks rose through the snaking curls of their hair.

I got dressed and ate the cereal that Sally had left on the counter. The television was on, playing a speech by the president. He was talking about a malaise. He seemed to be speaking right at me. His eyes were watery, dead, like Mama's eyes looked on the morning after Dad died, or Dawn's after she went down the hole. He said, "We can see this crisis in the growing doubt about the meaning of our own lives and in the loss of a unity of purpose for our nation."

Then the local newsman talked again about the killer. Last night he'd broken into another house, tied up the family, and sexually assaulted the mother. Then he murdered the family— the father and two young boys my age.

xii.

OUTSIDE, THE bonfire blazed. Hope danced around it, tossing in books, school papers, stuffed animals. A black tornado of ash spun up into the sky. Dawn didn't look at me, just went about tossing more things into the trash. I sat on the stoop and watched. Eventually there was nothing left to burn.

"Hope went in this morning," Dawn said, sitting down next to me. "Look at her, isn't she beautiful now?"

"I guess," I said. I looked at her out of the corner of my eye. Her black hair slithered around her face and over her shoulders. I looked down at her long legs and something stirred inside me. I thought about going into the guest room with her, crawling under the covers together. This thought made me sad, and seemed related to Dad dying, to the hole, to the malaise the president talked about, to the killer on the news.

"I know what you're thinking," Dawn said.

"No you don't."

"I wish he would come here, too," Dawn said.

"Who?"

"The killer."

"Why?"

"I want him to tie me up."

"Why would you want that?"

"Do you ever wonder what it would be like to die?"

"No."

"You're lying."

"No I'm not."

"Your dad died, didn't he? You didn't wonder what it was like for him?"

"No."

"I have a theory."

"What is it?" I asked.

"That it feels good. That the thing we're all afraid of actually feels good. Do you want to come with me?"

"Where?"

"The Void?"

"No."

"What if I promised you something?"

"What?"

"You can kiss me. You can touch me wherever you want."

xiii.

We waited until night. Sally came home and put on the TV. The entire news broadcast was devoted to the killer. The killings had gotten worse.

Dawn came to my room wearing her nightgown. It was made of moonlight. I could tell she had nothing on underneath. She took my hand and led me out of the room.

We passed by the TV. It painted Sally's face with dead electric light. A full ashtray smoldered next to her. For a moment, I thought she was dead. And then she lit another cigarette.

Outside, there were sirens in the distance, rising and falling like a baby's wails. The full moon's ashen light lit our way. Dawn suddenly wasn't a child anymore; she walked tall and queenlike. "It's like you can grab it and bring it down," she said, looking up at the moon's pitted face.

We passed into shadows. I caught a whiff of something from Dawn's hair or nightgown—fabric softener or shampoo—and it reminded me of Mama. I wanted to cry, to run home, to be anywhere else. I felt Dawn's hand in mine. For a quick second I thought it was Mama, leading me home, and that I was coming to the end of the dream. I'd wake, and Dad would be there, and Mama, and we'd all get in the car and go to the circus.

"Stop here," Dawn said, pulling her nightgown up over her head. I stood shuddering before her. The light fell in spatters across her breasts. They were shiny, like the baby dolls' plastic skin. "Take them off," she said, pointing at my pajamas. I looked down: Superman logos arranged in a pattern. I felt hot with embarrassment. "Do it," she commanded.

I stepped out of my pajamas. The warm ocean air felt weird on my skin. I covered my chest with one hand and my penis with the other. Dawn took both hands in hers and brought them to her hips.

"Have you ever done this before?" she asked.

"No," I said.

"Come on," she said, pulling me into my future.

xiv.

WE STOOD in the clearing. Moonlight washed everything, except for the Void which was as black as black can be. Something tapped my arm, and I saw small weightless pebble drift toward the hole.

"It's working," Dawn said.

"What is?"

"It was just waiting here all this time, started by someone else, but now we have to finish it."

"Finish what?" I asked.

Dawn pulled me to the ground. Stones bit my skin. She pulled my hand between her legs. Her private area was warm, moist; I felt it twitch like a frightened animal. Her black hair spread over me like a bat's wings. The moon grew in the sky until bursting.

I heard cracking, and the hollow scrape of concrete. Bits and pieces of the nighttime world drifted into the Void. Blades of grass shot like darts into its emptiness. Splinters of glass glittered as they sailed into the endless dark.

I felt us leave the earth. I saw Sally's house, light burning in the TV room. All the homes, up and down the street, with their blue television glow. I felt Dawn's hand on my penis, her slug-like tongue in my mouth. Was I dying, or was I more alive than I'd ever been? Was Dawn right—would it feel good to die?

Together, we went into the black. In the morning, we'd be born again to a world where killers would always be on the loose. Where presidents would never again remind us that our spirits had died, but only that we should be happy in death. We'd walk back into a place where baby dolls stayed baby dolls, and all the bright radiant things stayed frozen in time.

SWINDLER OF THE ABYSS

Level 1

THE GAMES were at the back, in a dark wood-paneled alcove that stank of cigarettes and cleaning fluid. There was a wrinkled *Children of the Grave* poster and a broken gum-ball machine and three old game cabinets and nothing else. I remember the games perfectly—the way they smelled, the cigarette burns like craters on the consoles, the red joysticks that had gone dull from too much play.

The place didn't have a name, just a red sign with black letters that said VIDEO STORE. It was in a strip mall whose parking lot we'd cut through on our way home from school. The owner was never there, and the guy that worked the counter—a college kid with no name and bad teeth—sat and watched videos and mostly didn't care how long we stayed or what we did. Kai and I would go there to rent R-rated horror movies and then we'd usually spend the rest of our money on games. My favorite was *Commando Brigade*. Kai always wanted to play *Doomslayer*.

Level 2

THIS OLDER kid Derek was usually there, racking up high scores on *Mutant Assault*. When we ran out of money, we'd watch him play. Derek had a mustache and a black leather jacket with a pentagram on the back, a crappy one he'd drawn himself with a paint marker. He was so good at *Mutant Assault* that he didn't have to think, and so he mostly talked to whoever would listen, which was usually Kai. Kai worshipped him.

"You guys watch porn?" Derek asked Kai one afternoon. His score on *Doomslayer* was over ten million. He was close to turning it over.

"Of course," Kai said, but I knew he hadn't. He'd payed a kid at school twenty bucks for a tape that turned out to be a bunch of Saturday-morning cartoons. To get back at him, Kai had stolen the kid's bike and dumped it in the pond.

VIDEO STORE would let us rent R-rated tapes, but we weren't allowed into the curtained-off area where the X-rated stuff was. We'd watch old sweaty men go in and out, and if we stood in just the right place by the rack of kids' movies, we'd catch a glimpse of pinkish box covers when one of the old guys slipped inside. Kai would get a boner. I mostly just felt weird in my stomach, like I'd eaten a spoiled sandwich.

"I saw one the other day," Derek said. "*Nightshift Nurses*. Hardcore."

"You own it?" Kai said.

"It's my dad's," Derek said. "He's got a whole stash."

"Can you copy it?" Kai asked.

"I only have one VCR. I can't dub tapes."

"What if I got you another deck?"

"I'd have to charge a hundred bucks a copy."

"A hundred bucks?"

"You could make a snuff film and sell it. I know someone who's been asking around for one of those. He was in here the other day."

"What's a snuff film?" I asked.

"A film where someone is murdered on camera."

Kai spent the rest of the afternoon buried inside himself. I could tell he was thinking about porn and money and snuff films. In those days, I was fine with just being a kid, but not Kai. There was always a next level. Last winter, it was making a copy of his dad's car keys so we could take joy rides. The summer before that, it was shoplifting rocket engines from Hobby Haven and lighting them off in the woods. Next thing you know, pyromania. We'd light fires and race home on our bikes as the sirens screamed around us. I should have known how it was all going to end.

Intermission

KAI HAD this weird, loping walk that made him look like a human that hadn't quite emerged from being an ape. His left foot turned inward, so he when he walked, he stepped mostly on the outside of his foot. He said it was the result of a birth defect—his foot got caught inside his mother when he was born, as if he refused to come all the way out. Because of his weird walk his sneakers were always worn down in crazy ways, and the rest of his clothes were torn and tattered to match. His parents had no money, so all his clothes were hand-me-downs. Any nice clothes he ever wore were shoplifted.

I didn't know how true this was—you could never tell with Kai—but he told people that his dick was bent just like his foot, and that when he got a hard-on it pointed off to the side. "When I fuck, I have to fuck sideways," he'd say, rocking his hips side to side. "Like fucking Elvis or some shit."

I knew Kai had never fucked anyone.

Kids at school threw food at him and pushed him into lockers and called him Kai the Caveman. I'd watch him get pushed around and see him almost about to cry and then something would harden inside his eyes and he'd brush it off and hobble away.

I didn't have it much better. I was no movie star. I had pimples and bad hair and a weak chin. I wasn't destined for greatness. I would never date a supermodel. No amount of staring in the mirror could convince me otherwise. But I did my best to avoid the bullies. Kai drew more attention than me and I always felt bad about this. When things went to hell, it was the one thing that kept me from telling him to fuck off.

Level 3

ON OUR way out, we rented *Dead Planet II* to watch at Kai's house, which is where we usually hung out if we weren't at VIDEO STORE. His parents were never home. There was always dried dog shit on the carpet in the living room, dishes in the sink, rotting food in the fridge. No one ever did any landscaping, so his backyard looked like a Vietnam War movie. There were small trees growing out of the house's gutters and no one ever took the garbage out.

I'd known Kai for three years and I'd never met his mom or dad. His older brother Vance did something with computers for a living, so his room was filled with keyboards and monitors and modems. Vance ran a BBS called Lost Objects. When I asked Kai what it was about, he said it was all about loneliness.

"But how can an online bulletin board be about loneliness?" I remember asking when he first told me. "Isn't the whole point that people talk to each other?"

"Yeah. They talk about how lonely they are."

The more I thought about it, the more sense it made. I had Kai, and he had me—we even talked to each other in real life—but we were both lonely. Loneliness was the thing that brought us together. Most kids at school had girlfriends, and played sports, and went to parties. If I'm being honest, I didn't even like Kai, I just ended up with him.

Bonus Round

I wasn't able to articulate it then, but it always felt like we were growing up at the end of something. Our days were haphazard, hollow. I'd often get a lump in my throat, on fall days when school crept up and the trees tossed off their leaves. Dread came in drips: the cork in my mom's wine bottle, a favorite show that turned out to be a repeat, the look on a cheerleader's face. I was crying inside, and so was Kai, but Kai bottled his tears and distilled them into rage. He egged us on, faster and deeper. Cheap thrills were expensive in the long run—they dulled you to real experience—but Kai didn't care. He wanted to feel something, anything, and I guess I did too. I was just too scared to do anything about it. Kai'd be the first to throw a rock through a window, and I'd follow. I can admit, it felt good, breaking things.

Level 4

It was under the bleachers where Kai first said to me, "We need to find a star for the movie."

I said, "What movie?"

"The snuff film, idiot."

"What are you talking about?" I asked.

He took a hit off his bowl and passed it to me. I took a drag. I could hear the distant referee's whistle and it filled me with emptiness. Someone had broken a beer bottle, and Kai was scraping one of the green shards along the palm of his hand, drawing blood.

"We need a star. Someone who'll die for us."

"No way."

"Don't be a fuckin' chicken shit."

I left him under there, cutting himself. It started to rain on the way home and I let it soak through me. I wanted to clean Kai off of me, wash the whole idea away. By the time I got home, I couldn't remember if he'd really said it to me or not.

Intermission

Kai collected Vance's theories and spouted them like they were his own. He said Vance told him that more and more of the world would eventually gather online, and they'd all become increasingly lonely and isolated. Vance believed that the message boards, which began as a "utopian construct," would devolve into "virtual ramparts" where people would isolate themselves against their enemies.

"And then, the whole world is eventually going to be like one big video game," Kai would tell whoever would listen, which was mostly me or Derek. "It'll be all about eliminating enemies and scoring points. And the reason most video games are about racking up scores and fending off invaders is because that's, like, human nature. Technology was created by humans so it's inherently reflective of our failures. Vance is writing a book about all this stuff—about the links between loneliness, technology and the apocalypse, or what he calls eschatology. It's gonna be called *A General Theory of Tears*. He's going to try to get it published, but if he can't he's just going to upload it to the BBSs as ASCII."

We'd hang out in Vance's room when Vance wasn't home, which was most of the time. The house sat dead and oblivious around us. We'd pick through the cables and cassettes, or thumb through the racks of floppy disks. We'd dial up Vance's 2400 baud modem and spend time on a few different BBSs. My favorite was Lady Hawk's Castle, where people talked about heavy metal and RPGs, but Kai looked at weirder stuff: boards about sex, or homemade drugs, or improvised weapons.

Eventually, we'd pop whatever we'd rented into the VHS deck and hope that the movie at least had some tits. *Dead Planet* turned out to not have any, and there wasn't even much gore. The movie was about a post-apocalyptic world where the ice caps had melted and most of the world's cities had drowned and the forests had burned away. The sets were cheap and the special FX were really crappy.

"This sucks," Kai said, ejecting the tape.

We went out into the yard and set off some firecrackers. Soon Kai went inside without saying goodbye, which was a sign for me to leave.

At home, Dad was in front of the TV and Mom was halfway through her second bottle.

Level 5

KAI TOLD me at school the next day that he'd bought a bunch of pot off of Dave Ferreti and was selling it for a markup. With the money, he'd buy a video camera to make the snuff film.

"How are you going to mark it up?" I asked. "Wouldn't they just buy pot from Dave?"

"I'm going to roll joints and dip them in formaldehyde. It gets you really fucked up."

"Sounds dangerous."

"Exactly."

"Where are you going to get formaldehyde?"

"Jay Mane. His dad's an undertaker. He's going to lift a jar for me."

"Just like that? Jay doesn't want anything?"

"I told him you were going to steal a porno mag for him as payment."

"Me? From where?"

"From The Brown Bag. You have to contribute to this shit."

"I don't know about this."

"Don't be a pussy."

Two days later, I went swimming and then into The Brown Bag carrying my duffel bag. When the guy at the register wasn't looking, I swiped a copy of Lesbian Lust. Heart doing somersaults, I payed for a Coke and then rode home on my bike in a daze. In my room, I stuck the porno between the pages of one of my Gorezone magazines. That night, with a flashlight, I jerked off to it into a wadded-up tissue.

I remember thinking about what came out when I ejaculated. Did it make my die a little bit inside? Did a bit of my life force seep out into the world, to be flushed away forever?

Level 6

THE NEXT day, at school, Kai passed the mag off to Jay, who hooked us up with the bottle of formaldehyde two days later. I helped Kai dip the joints at his house. We dried them on low in the oven and Kai said it made the house smell like a cross between a Grateful Dead concert and a funeral home. I told Kai he'd never been to a funeral home.

"Have to," he said.

"When?"

"Jay let me in to his dad's morgue once. There was a fucking dead body right there on the table."

"Bullshit."

He didn't fight me one it. He just glared at me and dipped another joint. Kai's line between what was real and what was fake was getting blurrier every day. If you told enough lies, did they come true? It made me think about the online message boards, and the things we both read there. How could we tell if anything anyone said was true? How did we even know if any of those people were real?

Who was Kai? Who was I? I wasn't sure I knew.

Kai sold three of the joints to Jeff Macomb the next day.

Macomb smoked one behind the bleachers and went running through the halls naked and screaming about an abyss at the bottom of everything, about demons in the phone lines, about mushroom clouds, about how we were all going to die. An ambulance came and took him away and nobody ever saw Jeff Macomb again.

Years later, I ran into a kid we went to school with. He said he'd seen Macomb on a street corner hitting a telephone pole over and over with an aluminum baseball bat. I pictured Kai instead of the pole, crumpled beneath the blows, begging for it.

Level 7

KAI LAID low for a while. Cops were poking around. We mostly hung at his house, leaving fake messages on the message boards, pretending we were girls, or old men, or angry guys wanting to start fights with people.

Kai would stick himself into a normal conversation—say, one where people were discussing the latest Make Believe album, or the new *Johnny Black* comics series—and he'd stir up shit, purposely try to turn people against each other. He spent long hours making pornographic pictures out of ASCII and pasting them into random places online. He stopped brushing his teeth. He stopped showering.

One afternoon, Kai put his arms around me and said, "You're my only friend." He was squeezing me a little too hard. He stunk of cigarettes and Jolly Ranchers and BO. I tried to pull away and he clamped his animal fingers around my wrist.

"Let go," I said. He dragged me over to his bed and slapped handcuffs around my wrist and to the bedpost. I screamed at him to let me out. He just laughed and said, "Why, so you can go home to your drunk mom? I'm keeping you here, slave."

He went into the other room and played video games on Vance's Commodore 64. I could hear him talking to himself, but couldn't hear what he was saying.

Intermission

FOR A while after that, I avoided him. I'd go straight home from school to the empty house. I started to feel our house was haunted, not by ghosts, but by me, by what I used to be and what I hadn't yet become. Somewhere in that afterschool spirit world drifted my future self, ruined by the things I would see and do. Ruined by Kai.

A few weeks went by. I got bored and started to miss Kai. I showed up at his house one Saturday and Derek was there. I'd never seen Derek outside of VIDEO STORE. They were both high as kites. Kai had his small VHS camera he bought with the formaldehyde pot money, and was filming the three of us. He pointed the camera in my face and offered me the joint they were passing around. I told him I didn't want any, and to get the camera out of my face.

"Faggot," Derek said.

"Pussy," Kai said.

"Shut up," I said.

"Are you scared?" Derek said.

"Keep going with what you were saying," Kai said to Derek, turning the camera on him.

Derek took a hit and held it and let out out a cloud and said, "Everything you see—all of this shit—everything we do," he said, waving the joint in a wild circle around the room, "is just a veil stretched over a fucking abyss, man. All the shit humans do: invent languages and science and shit—it just keeps the terror at bay."

"Terror of what?" I heard myself say.

"The unnameable."

They passed the joint to me and this time I took a hit. My head expanded to fill the room. I got totally paranoid. Both of them sitting there, across from me, some new unspoken bond forming between them. I remember thinking that maybe I'd be the star of the film. They'd get me messed up, take me out to the woods, and Kai would stick me with his dad's hunting knife while Derek filmed it. The part that scared me the most was that, deep down, maybe it's what I wanted.

"Yo, you're spacing out," I heard Kai yell at me.

"Sorry," I said.

"Are you fucking listening?" Kai said.

"Yeah, I'm listening," I said.

A dark feeling filled my stomach. Derek was explaining that the only defense against the unnameable terror was chaos magic. It was the avenue between the "symbolic order" and what "lies beneath"—chaos, primordial fear, grinning death. The way to combat chaos was not a futile attempt at control, but to inhabit the chaos itself, to take from it and to wield it, to accelerate everything toward the end. This was why Derek had been teaching Kai a set of rituals that they'd been performing in Kai's basement.

There was a heavy, silent minute where we all sat stoned and breathing, and then Kai looked at me and said, "Do you know that little pussy Shane at school? I'm going to enslave him. He's going to be the one. He's going to be the star of the fucking film. And the background to our movie? The end of this shit town. Everything burns."

"You have to be disciplined with this shit, asshole," Derek said. "If you aren't, who knows what will happen?"

They went on talking and I slipped out. As I left, they were drawing symbols on the floor with chalk. From outside, I heard Kai say, "I'll ask for a door. And when I go through the door, I'll find what I need. And I'll bring it back with me." I walked home through the sighing puddles to my haunted home. Dad was watching TV. There was just an empty bottle where Mom used to be.

Level 8

AT SCHOOL, there was an altercation between Shane and Kai. They were both called to the principal's office. Shane's parents got involved. Whatever had happened—whatever Kai had done or said—so concerned Shane's family that they had him pulled out of school and sent to the private Catholic school. Kai spent the afternoon in a rage. He turned his camera on me in the woods on the way home and ordered me to dance for him. I told him to fuck off. He just smiled and kept rolling. He trailed me all the way home, up the walkway, to my front door.

Level 9

A NEW game appeared at the back of VIDEO STORE. Kai was the first one to know about it. He'd evidently been there without me, which almost never happened. I didn't even know they swapped the games out, the old ones had been there so long.

"It's a weird one, I've never seen it before," Kai said. He was filming our walk—our feet, the pebbles sliding by, the sky, and, mostly, me.

"Get that camera off me. What's it called?" I asked as we cut across the parking lot.

"It's called *Swindler of the Abyss.*"

There weren't any cars in the strip mall's lot today, just pebbles and broken glass. I noticed the greeting card store next to VIDEO STORE had shut down, which must have happened in the last few days, because I could have sworn I'd bought gum there just last week.

"What's going on?" I wondered.

"Everything's going to shit and I don't care," Kai said. "I'm going to help it along."

Swindler of the Abyss stood where *Doomslayer* used to be, at the back of the game room, in the corner. It was an extra-large cabinet, one of the ones you could sit inside. The graphics on the side showed a long set of stairs descending through empty space. Far at the bottom was a pit of some sort, in which weird murky things bubbled.

Derek was there, already playing. He didn't say hi, didn't

even look at us, just went on pounding the game's shiny red button over and over. He looked possessed.

Kai shouldered in next to him, eyes electric. "Look at this," he said.

The game was first-person, and you stalked through a series of labyrinths with a machine gun. There was a quest element to the gameplay, though it wasn't immediately clear what you were supposed to be looking for. Instead of leading up, like in most games, the point was to go further down. Each level led to the next by a connecting stone stairway. The fighting grew fiercer the further down you descended.

"These graphics are awesome," Kai said.

"Next-level," Derek said. "16-bit, pseudo 3D, don't even know what the frame rate is."

"It looks real," Kai said.

Something about the game scared me. Its volume was turned up way too high, and gunshots echoed through the empty store. The kid at the counter wasn't there; we seemed to be alone. I noticed most of the tapes were gone from the shelves. The curtain to the X-rated section was gone, too. I left Kai and Derek and wandered inside it.

"Guys, come see," I said, but they didn't hear me. Outside, it started to rain. Thunder exploded across the empty parking lot. I didn't know what time it was.

I stood frozen among the racks. *Anal Bandits. Dungeon Desires. Colossal Cumshots.*

I remember hearing Kai say, "Yo, you have to see this. This must be it. There's a door on the side of this machine. Come on, help me move it."

I heard a shuddering sound, and Derek say, "Fucking open it up, pussy."

I picked up a copy of Gods of Pain. The large plastic clamshell box smelled like sex and chemicals and all the odors of the adult world. On the back, a woman with a red rubber ball strapped into her mouth was tied to a metal table in a dark room. A naked man wearing a leather studded hood stood over her.

"Guys!" I yelled again. It was quiet. Just the rain like teeth clicking against the store's window.

In a booming electronic voice, Swindler of the Abyss said, "Do you dare to come inside?"

I pulled myself out of the racks and noticed it was dark outside. Hours had gone by since we got there. I walked back into to the game room.

"Derek? Kai?" I called out. Swindler was pulled out from the wall, tilted toward me. I walked around to its other side. In the dark, I could make out a door in its side, large enough for a person to fit through. The door hung open. My eyes adjusted and I could make out the faint first steps of what looked like stone stairs, angling off into the dark. "Hey, guys?" I said, and my voice echoed inside the machine's darkness.

Level 10

I WAITED. I didn't know what time it was. I heard sirens outside. There was a fire somewhere, or an accident. Then, I heard footsteps. Kai and Derek climbed from the inside of the machine. Something had changed in their eyes. A detached, electronic coldness came off of them. It's the only feeling I remember from that day. They walked past me into the darkening night, taking our childhood with them.

Final Round

I GREW up, we graduated. Kai got left back. The future gripped us in its worried gaze. Summer invaded, quiet and without warning. Days stretched out. Hopes waned. Dad watched TV and Mom got drunk on weekdays and weekends both.

Something sour spread across the lawns and gardens. The streets grew rancid and dull. The news was filled with stories of murders and rapes and shootings. Homeless men pushed carts up and down the emptying streets. People moved away, leaving behind empty rooms and abandoned dreams. VIDEO STORE closed down, then the supermarket, then all the rest of it went dark

Mom asked Dad to leave. I saw little of him after that. Last I heard, he lived in a home, medicated and bald. I read books and found small hope in their pages, the hope that at some point, somewhere, the darkness might lift.

I'd see Kai here and there out of the corner of my eye, dead-faced, high on who knows what, in the woods, starting fires, huffing paint. That fall, I saw the news on TV: A local kid was arrested in the high school parking lot with a carload of guns and ammunition. Hooded, hands cuffed behind his back, head low in the cameras' lights, I could tell by the way he walked that it was him.

THE BREATH OF SATURN

i. Erich

THE DREAMS started when the men from the woods came and took me into the sky. Unlike common dreams—jumbled, indistinct—these were crystalline in form and charged with an urgency I can't express. In those years, I came to rely on them as a tourist depends on a guidebook. But there was always the risk of becoming too dependent. When there was no dream, I would falter.

Until the visit to the cabin that last summer, the dreams were always predictive of the most mundane circumstances: a visit to the department store, foreshadowed in the dead of night, or a phone call from an old friend, arriving with an anticipated jolt. Despite the dread the dreams instilled in me, in their utilitarian nature there was something I learned to rely upon.

During our time together, I never told Faye about the dreams and their oracular power. Almost masculine in her adherence to logic, she would have greeted them with a dismissive burst of air through her lips. The few other people I've described the dreams to have responded with meager scraps of interest. I'm not offended. These are private things.

It was the summer of '84. My parents were going through a divorce. I was six years old, lost in the shuffle. My father suffered a nervous breakdown and was hospitalized. On the phone he sounded shrunken, depleted. My mother, straining under the pressure, brought me to stay with my aunt and uncle, Jan and Fritz, at Willow Lake.

We traveled by car through the tired countryside. The larger buildings gave way to small clapboard houses, vast foggy fields, bails of hay like Paleolithic wheels in the mist. I had been to Jan and Fritz's once before, when I was a baby, but remembered nothing of the place as it unfolded through the window.

The adults conferred indoors. Through the spiderwebbed screen door I heard my mother say, "I don't know for how long." I stood on the ivied grass, among the siren of crickets, and waved goodbye as she drove off. It would be more than a year until I saw her again.

Fritz and Jan had a son named Gerard, who was crippled and walked with crutches. He wore thick Coke-bottle lenses whose temples resembled hockey sticks. Behind the glasses, Gerard's eyes were moist and swollen like overripe fruit. I remember how those eyes, slightly crossed, seemed to look not at me, but around me, as he leaned on his crutch and shook my hand. He smelled of rubbing alcohol, fabric softener, Band-aids.

Aunt Jan was a strict Christian, forbidding of all but the most wholesome activities. On several occasions, she smacked my hand with a ruler. On others, she sent me to the broom closet to sit alone in the moldering dark. These were minor infractions, things that back home I did without a thought. I soon learned to live a more pious life among the frogs and crickets. But at night I'd take the crucifix that hung on my wall and turn it upside down. I'd seen it in a movie.

Fritz was a quiet man who took me out in his paddleboat onto the odorous lake, with its brackish water and yellowing lily pads. We caught fish and I watched as he skinned them in the stinking garage. He'd tease apart the entrails as if divining the future. He often seemed on the verge of tears. He and Jan seldom spoke.

Gerard, too, was withdrawn. He'd sit in the yard most days, staring across the lake. Storms came and went. At night I'd listen through the window of the small screened-in porch that served as my temporary bedroom. The lake, the squabble of insects, the sweep of the wind in the leaves filled me with a feeling I couldn't place. It was as if those sounds were telling me something in a language I didn't understand.

"Don't go too far into the woods," Gerard told me one vacant afternoon. "It's not safe."

"Why?" I asked.

"You wouldn't believe me."

I AVOIDED Jan, and I stayed away from the woods. I spent my afternoons on the lake's boggy shore, skipping rocks, waiting for something to happen. One afternoon, three months after I arrived, a man came out of the woods. Naked, with skin as white as milk, he knelt before me. "We want you to help us," he said. His blue eyes shone like light through ice.

I wanted to run but my body was frozen. I heard myself say, "How?"

"Provide us with a body, and we will give you sight."

There was a sudden sound like a clap of thunder and we were aloft. Ashen clouds raced below our feet. Stars flared across the sky's speckled dome. Wind battered my naked body. "It is the breath of Saturn," the man said, pointing off into the black. I could make out seams along his arms and legs, as if his skin were really a poorly-made costume. There were others now, all identical to him: ashen skin, cerulean eyes, veins like anemone.

"You are just a body and a mind, and the two seldom meet," one of the others said.

"That's silly," I said, laughing.

"This won't hurt," one of the others assured me, as he pressed a cold needle between my legs. The pain was electric. Touching my forehead, they showed me a picture: a dark, sterile Earth, drained of life and color, wobbling like a weakly spun top at the edge of a cosmic abyss.

In the morning, I woke with a fever and sore throat. Gerard brought me tea. He asked me if I'd received a visit from the woods. "They took me," I said.

His eyes grew envious. For the first time they seemed to focus on me. "They didn't want me," he said.

I PASSED through the next three decades caught in a clairvoyant drift. The dreams alerted me to life's mundanities. I felt driven like a train, my years like rails through a dark mountain pass.

I had a talent for drawing, so found myself in the city attending an art college. This was a lonely, flat time. My feelings were suffocated, as if encased in concrete. The only student housing I could afford was in a low-rent dorm building that doubled as a halfway house for drug addicts. Transvestites roamed the damp halls in cheap wigs. Howls of withdrawal ripped through the building.

I spent my time alone, in thrall to the dreams' urgent vectors. If I dreamt of the supermarket, I'd find myself there the following day, among bruised fruit and electric light. If I dreamt of a museum, there I'd be, pulled in by the earthen tones of an Old Master, imagining myself as a painting hung on a wall.

No one can know what's it's like, to know life before it happens. All vitality is bleached away, like a book left in the sun. We don't realize that what gives us meaning is a constant clash with the unexpected.

In the winter of my third year, I had a dream, this one more vivid than most. I was in an unfamiliar apartment filled with dark figures. I couldn't make out faces. Music played, a dark pulse like the throb of internal organs. I wandered from room to room in search of windows, my only respite from the crowd. In each window I found framed the same repeated image: a steeple piercing a muddy sky. Their silhouettes, like sharpened bones, caused me to panic. Emerging from the dark crowd came a woman, dressed in white, heart beating like a piston. I sunk into her and woke with a feeling of deep fulfillment.

The following day, I was invited to a party by Jonas, one of the men in my building with whom I'd become acquainted. I was given an address on the outskirts, where the warehouses spilled shadows into stinking sewers. A drunk man answered the door. He introduced himself with a slur as Arturo. His unfocused eyes undressed me in the doorway.

Arturo explained that Jonas couldn't make it. I turned to leave but he pulled me inside and put a drink in my hand. The music was lewd. I couldn't breathe. I pushed my way through to a window. A stunning sense of déjà vu overcame me. Beyond the haze of the streetlights a steeple etched the smog. I fled along the wall, through limbs and sweat and spit. Another window, another steeple. Another, and another.

I had learned to listen to what the dreams said, to surrender the reigns to them. I reenacted the previous night's vision as a shaman performs a ritual. I retraced my steps with a rumbling dread. I turned from a window—the seventh church in the string of portents—and saw Faye swim from the dark like a pearl from an oyster's flesh.

ii. Faye

ERICH IS a dreamer. He has an artist's temperament, although he never made a career out of his talent. He is prone to lapses in attention, bouts of staring. I find myself asking him a question once, twice, three times before giving up.

I ask myself why I put up with it, why I've stayed with him all these years, and I don't have an answer. I don't believe in fate, or love at first sight. But there's something there inside him—dense, ferrous—that holds me in his orbit. It is as if we are meant to fulfill a prophecy together. Beyond this elusive gravitation, I am at a loss to describe our attraction.

Often, I recall our first meeting at the party in the city. How Erich appeared in the sickly light of a window, a church's black cross above his head like the blade of a guillotine. He seemed so lost, so alone. I like to think I rescued him that night. From what, I don't know.

✺

One of the things that binds us is Alan. When Alan was born, Erich seemed, for a time, to come alive. There was a purpose in his movements, a glimmer of meaning in his eyes. It was good, feeling like a family. We'd set out in the fall and speed through the season's changing colors. We'd pick apples, pumpkins, squash. We'd eat at a restaurant, the noise and chatter drawing us out of ourselves and into the world of people. All my life I've only wanted to be close to others, and yet I found myself in the orbit of two distant stars, in need of warmth and light but receiving only shadows and impressions.

Despite all that's happened, I can say that I trusted Erich with my life, that I loved him deeply. We flee into each other, human beings, hoping to find what? Immortality, joy in physical touch? Quiet nights made buoyant with low expectations, only togetherness.

Those first years were phosphorescent, but as Alan grew into himself, it became apparent that he was much like his father. Around the time of his fourth birthday, he grew moody, unsociable. I felt like the adhesive that kept Alan and Erich bound to the world, and prevented them from spinning off into their private worlds. Erich spent less time with Alan, Alan spent more time alone in his room, drawing pictures. The pictures grew increasingly strange: trees alive with purpose, white-faced men, labyrinthine diagrams that seemed to depict Alan's thoughts and nothing of the external world.

One summer, when Alan was six, I suggested we rent a cabin in the north. I thought of it as a way to draw us together, to recapture the sense of a family. I thought the exposure to nature would jog something in either Erich or Alan, and bring them out of their shells.

"In the woods?" Erich said. "I don't like the woods."

"You've never told me that."

"I didn't have a reason until now."

"I think it would be good for us."

ON THE morning we were to depart, Erich woke with a look that seemed inhuman, it was so filled with terror. I asked him what was wrong, and he replied that he had had a nightmare. He told me it was too terrible to recount.

The drive north was tense. Erich's dream hung in my mind, even though I knew nothing of its content. The droning of the tires on asphalt made me sleepy. The city gave way to the suburbs, and the low ranch houses surrendered to dark brush, fields, shadowy stands of oak and pine. Erich stared through the window with perspiration on his lip. He was in the grips of a silent panic. I had seen it before, but seldom this severe. I asked him if he wanted to turn back, and he shook his head.

Alan quietly read books, breathing heavily. He and his father seemed to be in emotional collusion, anxiety arcing between them like lightning. I cycled through the radio's dials, searching for something to alleviate the dread. I found only sad country, paranoid talk radio, dance music farmed from the cold valleys of microchips.

The cabin turned out to be much less desirable than the photographs let on. It was clear that no on had stayed in it for quite some time. The water in the toilets had left rings where it'd been sitting too long. Dusty magazines advertised publication dates years in the past. Spiders had spun elaborate cathedrals along the baseboards, in doorways, across grimy windows.

The place was set back in a dark wood. The backyard's deck jutted out over a thickly grown ravine. As we unpacked our things, Erich glanced uneasily at the window, through which the dark heads of pines danced.

"We'll make the best of it," I said.

Alan seemed drawn to the rear deck. Several times, after searching the house, I found him outside, at the weathered rail, staring off into the wilderness.

"What do you see?" I asked.

"So many trees," he said.

"Why do you look at them like that?" I asked, my hand on the nape of his neck. He was sweating, even though it was cool.

"I had a dream about them."

iii. Alan

I'VE ALWAYS been scared of Dad. Mom goes around the house doing things, cleaning, making our days brighter. She's always thinking about fun, making plans. If I'm a good boy she buys me a treat at the health food store: a vanilla shake, or a cookie. Dad is different. He stays in bed late, wrapped up in sheets like a baby. I look in the bedroom, in the morning, and I just see a lump. Sometimes he moans, roll arounds, even talks in his sleep.

I never told Mom that I see monsters. They're not like the ones in movies: these ones are quiet, skinny, and white like paper. But inside they aren't bright, or clean—they're black and big and empty like outer space.

Other kids at school draw pictures of airplanes, flowers, houses with Christmas trees and suns like lemon slices. I wear down my crayons trying to draw what I see in my dreams. It never comes out right. I crumple my pages up and throw them away. Mom finds them in the garbage and smoothes them out and hangs them on the fridge. "I like this one," she'll say, but I know she is lying. I hear it in her voice, shaky like one of Dad's old tapes that I play on his tape recorder. Once, I caught her looking at them and wiping tears from her cheeks. I don't want to make her sad.

I wish I was normal. I wish I didn't think the things I do.

One of those crazy thoughts—one I've never told Mom or Dad—is that I have this feeling that I'm not theirs. That maybe I got switched at the hospital, or that I'm adopted and they never told me.

When Mom said we were going up north, to a cabin in the woods, the first thing I thought about were the trees. Even though we'd never been there, I'd seen the trees before, over and over, in my dreams. When we pulled up to the house, I saw them peeking at me over the cabin's roof. They were saying hello, like we were old friends.

At the cabin, Dad was acting weirder than usual. He said he didn't want to go outside. Mom and I went for a walk while he stayed in bed. Across the dirt road was an old apple orchard. The sign was knocked down, and the trees were wild and knotted. The ground was covered with rotten apples. I picked one up and saw a worm wiggling its way through. The apple's inside was as white as bone.

While Mom made lunch, I explored the cabin. There were dusty empty closets, and an old iron fireplace, and board games that I wasn't old enough to play. When I asked Dad to play one with me, he said, "Not right now. Daddy doesn't feel good," and then went and stared through the window.

The backyard deck was covered in acorns and branches and dead leaves.

I spent hours back there. I wanted to jump up on the rail and dive into the trees. They were like a green ocean. It's like I'd been lost for my whole life and now I was home. This happened a lot, the funny feeling that I'd been somewhere before, even though I hadn't. When I told the other kids, they just looked at me and laughed and pointed. That's what they always did, they laughed at me.

It was in the night that Dad came and took me. My room was at the back of the cabin. I could hear the acorns falling on the roof, like little elves tapping with hammers and nails. I opened my eyes and Dad was standing at the edge of my bed. I couldn't see his face, only his hair, glowing with moonlight. I heard him sniffle, like maybe he was crying.

"It's time to go," he said.

"Where?"

"Out there," he said, pointing at the dark window.

"Why?"

"Don't ask why. Get up."

"Where's Mommy?"

"She's asleep."

"I want Mommy."

He came around the side of the bed and pressed his hand over my mouth. It smelled like mud and rain. I kicked at his arms but he pulled me out of bed and over his shoulder. We went through the door and into the main room. It smelled staticky, like when you rub a piece of styrofoam across your sleeve.

He put me down and knelt in front of me. I could see now he was definitely crying. "Are you listening to me?" he whispered.

I nodded.

"You're going to come with me. Do you understand?"

"No."

"They've been waiting all this time. Ten years is a long time, Alan."

He took my hand and led me down the long dark hallway to the back door. There were baskets and blankets and paddles and oars nailed to the wood panelling. Paintings of lakes, boats, hills and trees, all nailed this way and that. We passed by the rumbling dryer. I thought of Mom and I felt sick: all the things she did for us. For me. For Dad.

I stopped and pulled. Dad growled and pulled me off my feet. He dragged me the rest of the way as we banged through the screen door.

The night was loud. A billion bugs screaming. "Do you hear it?" Dad asked as we went down the deck's stairs into the trees.

"What?"

"Panic. The whole world, every living thing: in a panic.

No one knows what will happen next. I want to feel that. I've never felt it before."

"I want Mom."

"Stop it."

"Where are we going?"

"Quiet," he said, as we crunched through the dark. Dead branches snapped like bones. Animals ran through the dark. The crickets were so loud I covered my ears.

"Where are we going?" I moaned.

"You know I love you, right?"

"No."

He stopped. I couldn't see. For a while we stood there. I could hear his breathing over the crickets. Then we started walking again. My feet and lungs hurt. My eyes adjusted. We were on a path.

"This way," Dad said. "This is what I dreamt."

We climbed. The air got colder. I started to cry. My heart beat faster. I realized, in the dark, in the woods, that I didn't know Dad. He was just a guy who slept, woke, walked from room to room, carried heavy things for Mom, never said anything to anyone about how he was feeling, what he was thinking. I realized he had this whole life, inside his head, apart from us. And whatever was happening right now was his way of getting away from that life, or maybe going deeper into it.

We came to a hilltop without any trees. Across the way, the treetops were like heads with messy hair in the wind. The moon was huge, flat, stuck on the sky like a glow-in-the-dark sticker.

Dad pushed me out under the wind and the stars. I felt his hand brush my shoulders, my back, and then I heard his footsteps running away behind me through the twigs and leaves. I tried to move but I was frozen. A cold wind came down off the trees and across my face. My tears were icicles. I wet myself, and it felt warm, and nice, and good. And then he came out of the trees. A man with skin like the moon. A man with stars for eyes.

THE PUNCTURE

It took two months before I could bring myself to enter Don's studio. When he was alive, I was forbidden to enter, so cleaning it out felt like a betrayal. The studio's arrogant metal door sat between me and what remained of my beautiful Don. On some nights I sat outside it, listening, as I'd done for years. When I couldn't bear it, I'd go out wandering the streets, inhaling the sewer fumes, the stench of garbage, the rot and decay. I was trying to get closer to Don.

By the time I gained the courage to go in, I'd already removed all traces of him from elsewhere in the house. His photographs were the first to go: The nudes, the still lifes, the optical illusion pieces he'd won awards for. I took what little clothes he had to Goodwill. The books were harder to part with; books on magic and the occult, first editions of De Sade, Nietzsche, Bataille—the entire underbelly of literature, boxed and dispersed like Bibles to be discovered by the city's other lost souls.

The banal things proved the most terrifying to dispense with. His toothbrush. His pack of antacids on the shelf by the door. His shoehorn. The boxes of his favorite sugary cereal tossed like the next day's confetti into the trash.

Toward the end of his life, Don alluded to the fact that he'd discovered something that changed the course of his work. He said he was done with photographing reality as we knew it—that the optical illusion pieces had been the beginning but, because they were "mere trickery," were ultimately dissatisfying as works of art.

It was around this time that I found piles of his old photos in the trash. He grew jittery, suspicious, more despondent than usual. He spoke about magic and its relationship to art and loss.

He was spending long hours in the studio and less time with me. His sex drive disappeared; his appetite dried up. I knew not to pry—it was the quickest route to an argument—but I gently nudged him about this discovery. He said it had something to do with "the abyss" and his attempt to photograph it.

It was around this time that I began to suspect that he had a drug problem. I dug through his drawers, scoured the apartment for clues. But whatever he was doing, he had confined it all to the studio. It was there that I'd find whatever had become of Don.

IT TOOK a half pint of whiskey before I could touch the knob. Finally, with a heaving sob, I threw open the door to all that was left of him. I switched on the light expecting him to be standing there, pulled like one of his images from an emulsion of tears and grief.

The room tilted. A gale of sorrow blew me to the floor. I was falling and the room's floor was the wall of a pit I was struggling to climb out of. I pulled myself to my feet and took stock: In the center of the room ran two long metal tables crowded with cameras and lenses and canisters of film. Along the wall closest to me stretched a workbench where he repaired his equipment. At the far side, one lonely window looked out onto the wall, mere feet away, of the neighboring tenement: colorless bricks, a few pipes, another darkened window.

Underneath the window sat a case of thin metal drawers where he stored his prints. Finally, huddled in the corner was the small jury-rigged darkroom, fashioned out of plywood and black paint, where he'd taken his life.

I circled the room with weak knees. Everything would need to be broken down, priced, listed on auction sites. I pulled back the darkroom's curtain, hesitated, and then forced myself inside. I stood in the silent blackness and wondered how many times Don had done the same. Day after day, year upon year, he'd come in here, knowing I was outside, waiting for him to return. Until finally, one day, he didn't.

Love, as I've known it, is a mutual recognition of lack. It is not plenitude, although it feels as such—this is the trick it plays. Each of us walks through life with a hole in the shape of a person, a puncture from which our life-force escapes. We search desperately for someone to plug this leak. We meet another person with whom our emptiness overlaps, and both fall into the illusion that two negatives make a positive. This high-wire act carries many people to the end of their days, but often enough they come crashing down, reacquainted with privation.

Don was a master of illusion. His photos were some of the more incredible pieces of visual trickery the world has known. But a pretended fulfillment—from me, from his work—was one illusion he couldn't conjure. But for my sake, he tried. Even if he wasn't always present, I know he loved me, in his distant way. I wasn't a masterpiece, but I was at the very least an excellent forgery. Sometimes, this is more than enough.

I STARTED with the cameras, noting the make, model, and condition of each, and placed them into boxes. There were large-format ones, antique ones, small point-and-click ones. One of the last was a child's toy camera—a plastic, rainbow-colored thing that produced Polaroid-style prints of surprising quality. I realized the device had some film left in it, and I snapped a photo of the studio and took it with me, closing down my operations for the day.

In the kitchen, I pulled a frozen dinner from the freezer and placed it in the microwave. I set the toy camera's print down to develop. It took several minutes for the photo to come to full clarity. When it did, I recognized the strange pigmentation of the print; Don had taken many photos with this toy camera, some of which had hung on our walls.

I stared at the photo of the empty studio as I ate my lonely dinner. There was something off about the image the toy produced. Not just the colors were skewed, but the perspective was as well. The cheap lens had warped the room's surfaces, bent them into impossible angles. I grew nauseated reliving my fall to the studio's floor. I turned the print upside-down and finished my dinner in silence.

DON WAS a secretive man. In our relationship, he was physically generous—except for our last months, sex was always passionate—but outside of bed he was emotionally reserved. In conversation, he'd go into passionate detail about films, works of art, novels—but rarely strayed into the minefield of his own feelings, which I knew to be volatile.

His past was a blank space, yet he knew mine in significant detail—my Midwestern small-town upbringing, my closeted romance with an older man when I was eighteen, my failed attempt at becoming an artist. When we first met, he grilled me about my history in the way a journalist interviews a subject. And I spilled it all for him, eagerly. Don was like that; you wanted to tell him everything, even if he offered very little in exchange.

All I knew about Don's childhood was that his mother died of ovarian cancer when he was a boy, and that his alcoholic father was neglectful, most likely abusive. Further details were scant. When his father grew ill with Alzheimer's, Don made a single trip to his childhood home to take care of some last things. He returned pale, preoccupied, more distant than usual. I asked him what it was like, being there.

"Walking through those rooms," he replied, "I felt like the ghost of someone who was murdered in that house."

"I'm so sorry," I said. And he looked up at me, tears in his eyes. "Talk to me, what happened back then?" I asked.

"I can't," he said.

"You're like an island," I told him.

"I don't want to be."

"Well, come back to me then, I'm here."

"It doesn't work that way. You'd have to be stranded with me, and you don't want that. Besides, island is the wrong metaphor."

"I don't want to get literary."

"It's like there's a space—back there, in that house, inside me—that I can't access. I can only describe the contours, get right up to the edge, but whatever's inside is missing."

"I don't understand," I said. "Do you not remember? Do you not want to remember?"

And instead of helping me understand, he went into his studio to work.

THINKING BACK, I remembered when I'd first seen the toy camera. Don had brought it back with him from his trip home to take care of his father. And it was soon thereafter that he'd embarked on the ultimate phase of his work. The phase that most likely killed him.

I picked up the toy again and examined it. It was scuffed and discolored. Decades-old grime clung inside its crevices. Most likely the camera had been Don's as a child. I turned it over in my hands and then I found them: in faded marker, on the underside of the camera, his initials—D.A., written in a child's unmistakable hand.

I thought of young Don, alone in a house I'd never been to, living a meager life I was only dimly aware of, coexisting with a man who'd stolen a piece of him, leaving behind a wound he kept hidden from me for all those years.

I looked at the photo again. With fresh eyes I realized that it wasn't an artifact of the cheap lens that had bent the room into its strange appearance—the room itself was misshapen. The entire space tapered, funnel-like, toward the window, with its ugly view of the tenement wall.

I left my dinner and stood again at the door of the studio, peering in. I realized I'd done this countless times with Don himself, attempting to look inside, trying to locate clues.

I thought of his moods, and how I'd written them off for so many years as a typical artist's temperament. "Don's an artist, and all artists are moody," I'd say at parties, and we'd all laugh. Except for Don.

What is a mood? When Don was in one, he went somewhere else, as if having an out-of-body experience. He'd be with me physically—eating dinner, watching a late show, having a cocktail—but his mind would be elsewhere. I assumed he was thinking about his work and forgave him for his remove. An artist was always working. But perhaps he wasn't just elsewhere in space, but also in time. Back to Don-the-child, clutching his toy camera, wielding it like a weapon against terrors great and small. Don running through the empty lots, alone—he told me often he had no friends growing up—escaping inside the lens. Don, doing as he learned to do, framing pictures as an antidote to pain.

I recalled a passage of an essay he had written for a photography magazine: "Composing a photograph is not about what is in the frame, but what is left outside. Our gaze is drawn not to the photograph's ostensible subject—whatever it may be—but to what lies just beyond the edge. We, the viewers, look not to see, but to be prevented from doing so."

Turning these words over, I realized that the subject of all of Don's work was something beyond the edge of not only the viewer's awareness, but of his own.

In I went again, this time armed with foreknowledge of the room's strange geometry. The original dizziness returned, but this time I knew it wasn't only grief; that the floor canted like a shipwrecked boat toward the lone window, with its gray view of the tenement building's wall.

I steadied myself. The strange distortion in space folded everything toward the window, which drew me like an iron filing to a magnet. I approached it slowly. As I grew closer, I realized that the perspective through the wall's lone window—the angle of the bricks, the hard edge of the shadow, the other window's sill—did not change as I walked.

And then it struck me that what I was looking at was an optical illusion. Pasted over the window was a life-size photograph of what was the window's view to the outside world. It seemed to me to be one of Don's last, great tricks. But had he put it here to be played on me, or on himself?

Don had composed the photo in such a way as to make it convincing from whatever position someone happened to be standing in the small room. It helped that it was a narrow room, with not many vantages available from which to view the illusion.

I leaned in closer to inspect the image. It was, in typical Don fashion, a beautiful piece of work—clear, vivid, almost hallucinatory in its replication of real-world light and shadow. I stuck my fingernail under the lower-right edge of the image and began to peel it back. No light emerged. I peeled some more, and all I could make out was black. Perhaps he'd darkened the window to keep out the light. But he had his darkroom for that purpose. I pulled the rest of the image from the window and let the large curled photo drop to the floor.

I found myself standing before a pure black pane of glass, like a spacecraft's portal into starless space. An emptiness came over me, and with it a stunning confusion. Whatever had gone on in here, in Don's final days, was much stranger than I'd imagined.

I unlocked the window's clasp and pulled on the sash. At first, like most old windows in city buildings, it didn't budge. I pulled harder, and with a loud screech the sash came up. From behind me, I heard a nervous rumble, and then a loud crash. A camera slammed to the floor. A few small plastic film canisters sailed past me through the window into the abyss beyond. I heard the girders of the room croak, and particles of plaster floated past me into the dark.

Language comes up short when I attempt to describe what I was looking at. To refer to it positively, as an object—a void, a hole—was to suggest it was a thing when it was in fact no-thing. What I was standing before was a negation of the tangible world. I felt it pull on my insides, beckoning me to enter. I tugged myself from its orbit and fled the room.

I SAT on the sofa and thought about how staring into that emptiness, I'd felt closer to Don than I'd felt in all the years I'd known him. And this feeling was compounded by another— that I hadn't known him at all. I'd only seen the scaffolding, Don's attempt to erect an artifice over a wound, to stretch a drumhead over an abyss, to frame a photo of desolation and pass it off as himself.

I went to the bar and fixed two cocktails, as I'd done almost every night when Don was alive. I placed one of Don't favorite jazz albums on the record player and set it lightly spinning. I toasted to the ghost who sat with me, more present now than he'd ever been in flesh and blood.

With whiskey in my veins, I reentered the studio. I could be a venturer too—I could be an artist if I wanted to be. I took the toy camera and strapped it over my shoulder. I climbed atop the metal chest of drawers in front of the window. Behind me, the whole apartment sagged toward the vacuum's planetary pull.

I placed one leg through, and then another. I dipped my head under and then perched on the sill, looking out. The long, fathomless dark sat silent and endless before me. Shadows moved in shadows. All the physical objects of the world were stripped of meaning. I was hit by the shining awareness that not just art, but everything we do, is an attempt to put a frame around a void.

I dangled my legs like a child. How far would I fall? Would I rise? Would I float? Would I approach an event horizon, and discover Don there, snapping pictures of our emptiness? Would he be fulfilled, finally, in the recognition that there was nothing more to skirt around, no wound left to conceal? Would he reveal to me his reason for fleeing so soon from life? Or would I kiss him, and take him inside me, and be content with never knowing why?

THE INNKEEPER'S CHILDREN

I HAVE nowhere to go, so I travel north. I pass through desolate manufacturing towns with their radioactive rivers, the drug-ravaged neighborhoods abandoned by grace. I drive up out of the forsaken cities, across the bridges into wilder territories. The villages—arcane smatterings of old warehouses, lean-tos, and dollar stores—instill no hope in me. Between these meager signs of civilization stretch endless forests, dim and ignorant. The land has seen better days.

I'M NOT sure what I am hoping to find. Perhaps I am looking for a home. All my life I have never felt like I belonged. I've always carried this sense of estrangement with me, but from who or what I can't say. Maybe what I seek is a lost piece of myself. It is possible it's a part I never had.

I SLEEP beside the pumps of an abandoned filling station. I dream that the emissaries of a race of aliens descend from the star-specked sky. Their chariot touches down in the bruised grass. I am their first contact, I who know no one, am of no importance, have nothing to offer other than a longing to be stolen away.

THE NEXT morning, the humdrum light reveals no signs of celestial visitation, only the same crumbling traces of human activity. I wash my face in an oily brook and drive on. I come to a place called Egypt. The town center holds no shining pyramids, only silent warehouses, a cockeyed tavern, a shop selling X-rated books and videos. I find a greasy spoon at the edge of nowhere where I order breakfast. I can't bring myself to eat; the waitress doesn't look me in the eyes. I want to ask her what hardships she endures, what she dreams of at night. If she, too, longs to be taken up into the starry sky like royalty.

I'LL TELL you about myself. I'm fifty-two years old, unemployed, never married, no children, no family to speak of other than Mother. More than halfway through life, I remain a virgin. Meeting women has always been difficult for me. I had a girlfriend once, a lifetime ago. Her name was Sophia. For a few awkward months we held hands, went on walks, exchanged hesitant kisses on her back porch in the summer. I remember the feeling well—I was losing Sophia before I had her. Loss was embedded in my very experience of her. Sure enough, she eventually grew tired of my lack of nerve. I let her fall, afraid to hold on.

SINCE THEN, Sophia has become a prominent figure in my dreams. As her dream-self, she has not aged. In one scenario, I am a freedom fighter in a war-torn land where I rescue her from encroaching danger, my heart on fire with pride. In another dream, she is only a coy shadow that I chase through the rooms of a ruined house. Often, she is not a person at all, but an enveloping, otherworldly presence which exudes a warmth and safety beyond words.

I visit the X-rated video store. I skulk through the bright, prying light. There is a peculiar odor of cheap ink, cardboard boxes, something else I can't place. There is another man here. Our eyes meet for a moment and we form an unspoken bond. We are both fallen angels. I purchase a magazine with my dwindling cash and drive North out of town.

I turn onto a forgotten dirt road beside a crumbling cemetery. In moon's glow, I masturbate among the graves. The taciturn light reveals the headstone of a small child, dead at seven years old, a century ago. I shed a tear. I imagine my fluids mixing below ground, seeping through root and soil to touch her immortal remains. Reconstituted, she clambers through the ground and rises to a better world where people are never lonely and children never die.

My shyness isn't the only reason for my virginity; there is something about sex that poses a terrible threat. My ego has always felt vulnerable to dismantling, as if my identity is a child's toy that came with the disclaimer SOME ASSEMBLY REQUIRED. And, all those years ago, when I opened the box, there were no instructions, only a mess of pieces that didn't fit together. I sensed this threat of collapse strongest when in proximity to women. There is a raging wind that comes from them. Sex is a cyclone come to blow my house down.

I leave the cemetery and drive on. I pass the hulking backbone of a landfill and imagine it prying itself from the bitter earth and lumbering off, trailing tendrils of trash in the night. I arrive in another town, one with no name. In the radiance of a liquor store's neon, I recognize the waitress. She is wearing makeup, leather boots, a short skirt. I roll down my window and she leans in, her face haloed with neon light. I realize now that she resembles my Sophia. She asks me what I want, and I tell her I only want to take her away from this bleak street corner and to a warm bed. She takes this request as an affront, but I offer her more money than she'd make doing more unspeakable things.

WHEN I left mother, she cried. She said that the world was much too harsh for someone like me. We stood together in my room, among the detritus of my boyhood, and I expressed regret. She asked me where I thought I was going. I told her anywhere but here. She moved to put her arms around me and I pulled away—the first time I'd ever done so. At the beginning of my journey, I felt her sitting by my side, judging me. Disapproval, consternation, a ladle of shame into my cold poison soup. These were the ingredients by which I'd been made.

WE DRIVE up into the meager hills. The waitress says she knows of an inn where we can spend the night. I must do what's expected of me by my conscience. I can rescue her from corruption and breathe fresh life into her. My kindness will inspire a transmutation that will ripple across the broken land and resuscitate the dying world.

THE INN is a downtrodden structure at the end of a gravel drive in a dismal wood. With my first glimpse, a curtain falls over my dream of renewal. As we draw closer, I notice the inn's crumbling dormers converge at odd angles, as if put together by a blind child's hands. The design of its stories betrays an ignorance of balanced ratios. Paint peels. Wood rots. Windows sit at erratic intervals. I remark to the waitress that the inn looks all wrong, but she merely laughs and pulls me inside.

THEY HAVE built the entrance lobby with a disregard of human proportions. The ceilings tilt at sickly angles. The chairs and tables are too large or too small; some sit smashed to pieces. I imagine a consortium of dwarfs and giants occupying the inn, plotting a takeover of the human realm. From deeper inside come the sounds of incessant sawing and hammering. We approach the front desk. An elderly woman looks up from a yellowing guest register. She seems suspicious of our intentions. I assure her we are only looking for a place to rest. The woman hands us keys to a room and warns us not to disturb the innkeeper. He lives on the top floor, in a room directly above our own.

AS THE waitress leads me through the halls, I am overcome by the feeling that I've been here before. When I was a child Mother would take me on trips to the North. We stayed in this place, I am sure of it. My déjà vu strengthens as we pass deeper into the inn's halls. I picture my mother and I, alone together. A yearning for better days overtakes me. What hopes I'd had, how ignorant I'd been. But the place I remembered wasn't like this, with its stained and threadbare carpet, the ceilings spidered with cracks. A layer of dust coats everything. And beneath it all—the endless hammering.

AS WE climb to our room, Sophia tells me the story of the inn. The area was once home to several booming mining towns. The innkeeper, a speculator, was the heir to a copper fortune. When the land had been stripped bare, the mines were abandoned, and the towns fell into poverty. The innkeeper had the idea to erect a beautiful inn. People would come from far and wide to experience it. But the innkeeper fell ill, and his three children inherited his fortune. Fancying themselves architects, they set about building the inn according to their own plans. In their ignorance they built an embarrassment. As the innkeeper's condition worsened, his children's hubris grew.

We unlock our room and step inside. My eyes go to a hole in the ceiling, from which a putrid liquid drips. The night's bitter breeze leaks through a cracked window. The waitress takes off her clothes. She has been here before, perhaps a hundred times. The room's disrepair doesn't faze her. She is part of it. In her nakedness, she stands before me, an attempt at perfection among the debris. She steps closer and I pull away. She asks what's wrong. I tell her everything is wrong, can't she see?

She puts her hands between my legs. I wither. Then, footsteps. I glance up and Sophia's eyes follow. It is the innkeeper, pacing. She puts her arms around my neck and brings her lips toward mine. Something seizes inside of me. She feels it too.

She pulls back and peers into my eyes. I tell her I must know more. There is nothing more to know, she replies. I tell her I need to know what's wrong with the innkeeper. He is a very sick man, she tells me, but he once was healthy and beautiful. She should know, she assures me, because she was once his bride-to-be. A fearful jealousy seizes me. A bodily cry echoes somewhere in my hollows. Sophia collapses into the bed and goes to sleep.

I LEAVE her in my shame. At the front desk, I demand to see the innkeeper. I complain about the terrible leak, the hole in the ceiling, the smashed window, the dirt and the grime. The woman explains that the innkeeper sees no one and that I must speak to his eldest son. She says I can find him in the furnace room, where he is doing repairs.

I TAKE the elevator down. From beyond its tarnished door, I hear the clanking of machinery. It opens, and I am greeted by dank, scorching air. I stalk a dark cinderblock hallway. Pipes hiss like snakes. The walls seep a whitish, foamy liquid. At the end of the hall, I see the crimson glow of the furnace room. I hear the grunting and groaning of an animal in heat. I peer inside. On the concrete, in a black hissing puddle, is Sophia, pinned by the pulsating flesh of the innkeeper's son. On his arm is a tattoo of a lump of coal. The lump slips molten over his rippling muscles. Sophia sees me and smiles. Her eyes are dull diamonds. I stare in shock at both of them. Fused together, they resemble an insect with too many arms and too many legs. From this confusion of limbs, I hear Sophia cry, or laugh, or scream.

I RUN up, out of the heat and dark. Dust rains from the ceiling. The inn cants like a boat in a gale. The woman at the front deks has grown older. She is frail, papery, a whisper of a person. The guest register is bloated beyond proportion. Suddenly, crowds of people are flooding into the inn. I demand to see another of the innkeeper's children. The woman, who can no longer speak because her teeth have spilled to her feet, points to a door at the end of the hallway.

I SHOULDER past the crowd and pound on the door. A man in a fine suit opens the door. His hair is oiled, his teeth are like pearls. I insist he hears my complaints. He ushers me into a shining office, lined with brass and leather and mahogany. On his desk sits an accounting ledger. The man stands across from me and asks me what the trouble is. I tell him what I've seen—the hole and the cracks and the dust and the discomfort. He tells me he has a business to run, can't I see? He leans toward me and ensnares with his eyes, two voids where I am for a moment suspended. He opens his mouth and through gold teeth hisses, "Look at yourself, you are the problem."

I LEAVE him and walk further down the hall. I find another door and push through it into a room filled with mirrors. Oval, floor-length, large and small—all aglitter like the afterlife. I see myself echoed and split, a crowd of the undead. Everywhere I turn—my face, my guilty eyes. At the center of the room, on a red velvet carpet, sits an elegant woman. Her face is caked with makeup. Bottles sit like runes at her feet—perfumes and lotions and unguents. Beneath the woman's painted face, her skull shudders and collapses. I watch her peel back her skin and, with a pair of glimmering tweezers, press the bones back into place. With a sound like a crushed melon, she slips the skin back over her skull. She says, "Look at yourself, you are the problem."

I RUN and I climb. The inn rumbles. Shards of plaster explode at my feet. Walls collapse. I pass the ballroom and peer inside. I see Sophia waltzing alone, drunk, naked. A thousand men sit licking their animal lips. I grab her by the wrist and tug her toylike through the collapsing world. Her head lolls. Her tongue snakes. "They want me, they want me," she repeats. I drag her up stairways and ladders. I can sense the innkeeper nearby. When I see him, I will demand an explanation. I will demand reparations. I will demand knowledge.

UP WE climb. Sophia drags behind me. The stairs grow dark and narrow and end in a small door. Much too narrow for who should be inside. I push and the door swings open. On my hands and knees, I crawl through and pull Sophia, now just a plastic doll, behind me.

I AM back where I belong. This is the place that's always been there, behind everything, above everything. My crib and my dresser and my chest of toys. Mother says, "You'll feel better in no time, you are a sick child, and a sick child needs his mother." I clutch my doll, Sophia, her plastic skin worn from too much love. I am both young and old. Why does she keep me here? I look around at all that I've lost, all that I've gained. Mother paces. It is not only her feet I hear above me, marking time, but my own. She has broken open a hole at the top of the world, and teaches me to listen through it. She believes she has provided me what I need in in order to build a place to live. If only she'd known her plans were faulty. If only she'd known she took more than she gave.

WEDNESDAY'S CHILD

"When modes of expression are worn out, art tends toward non-sense, toward a private and incommunicable universe."
—E. M. Cioran

AFTER THE divorce, Clay moved into an apartment on the far side of town, where the rent was cheap. The trees were scarce, the sidewalks cracked and buckled. Exhausted homes, some derelict, refused to give up their shadows. Through the eastern-facing windows, smokestacks smeared tendrils across the low sky. Out on the boulevard, outmoded men clung to the doors of liquor stores, squinting at lottery tickets. The dollar shops, with their defeated aluminum awnings, seemed to thrive, although he rarely saw anyone come or go. He kept his shades drawn. At night, he'd drift off to the sound of vagrants breaking bottles in the alley. It sounded like wind chimes in the dead air.

WITH THE new apartment came a recurring nightmare. Abbie, Bradley, and he were seeing a summer blockbuster on opening weekend. The theater was labyrinthine, constructed of impossible corners and blind alleys. He had tickets, but couldn't read what they said. Hallways led to grimy restrooms; doors opened onto dead-ends. The movie was starting and they were going to miss it. Bradley's hand in his felt wormlike and malformed. Abbie hovered at the periphery, a drifting cloud of ideas: nonchalance, condescension, indignation. When they finally arrived in the correct auditorium, it had too many screens, all too distant to see. They ranged through cockeyed rows with nothing to bind them but their confusion. He'd wake from this dream with a sense of unimaginable loss.

His apartment sat opposite a public school, a tomblike building flanked by ruptured asphalt fields. They had built the place when teachers still cracked pupils across knuckles with yardsticks. On weekends, the rusty swings creaked in the wind that came up off the lake. When the children let out for recess, he plugged his ears to dampen the screams. He recorded them on his phone and played them back at night, after the alcohol had soaked in. He slowed the shrieks down, filtered out specific frequencies. He didn't know what he was hoping to find.

The judge ordered that he could see Bradley every other weekend, and the last Wednesday of the month. The first time his mother dropped him off she asked, "Are you sure it's safe?"

"This is where I live," Clay replied.

"Don't let him go anywhere," she warned, and sped off.

"So, what do you want to do?" he asked the boy.

"I don't know," Bradley said. Just then the recess bell rang, and they both turned to the schoolyard, with its high chain-link fence topped by coils of barbed wire. "Why do they have barbed wire?" Bradley asked as the doors burst open and the screaming children bled out onto the asphalt. "To keep child molesters out?"

"Maybe to keep the children in," Clay answered.

Bradley was homeschooled; it was Abbie's decision. On his visits, the boy brought her curriculum with him, but he often finished his work before Clay had a chance to help. Instead, they worked on a puzzle—a colorful ocean scene with schools of fish among an efflorescent coral reef. "All the reefs are dying," Bradley said one afternoon. Clay didn't know how to respond—he was a member of the adult world which had poisoned the skies and filled the oceans with plastic.

"At least we have the puzzle," Clay said.

When they got to the end, they realized there were pieces missing. Bradley sulked in his room. Clay turned on the TV.

At the time, he was working from home as an editor for a small regional consultancy, polishing business argot. Over the years, he found he'd gotten very good at taking nonsense and giving it a credible sheen. His work turned out best when he ignored the meanings of the words and focused on their phonetic qualities. They formed a kind of hysterical poetry, a panicked attempt to bend language to the demands of the technological age. Clay saw his job as not to humanize this lingo, but to push it deeper into unintelligibility. He knew his job was done when the prose slipped into pure, ecstatic gibberish.

Clay had once harbored dreams of becoming a novelist. After Bradley was born, the fervent creative field he'd cultivated dried up like a desert. Instead of taking this catastrophe in stride, he pretended it wasn't happening. He stoked the engine of a growing resentment. He fueled this machine with beer and television and pornography. Abbie grew unhappy; Bradley, neglected. He was bitter toward them not just for the time they siphoned, but for the contentment they brought. Abbie sent him packing, along with the unopened gift of their love.

When Clay was a child, he'd come late to language. He remained mute well beyond the age when other kids had uttered their first words. His parents bounced him between doctors, psychologists, and speech therapists, all who could find no explanation. His mother told him that when the words eventually came, they arrived in a torrent. "At first you wouldn't talk, and then I couldn't get you to shut up," she'd joke. When she first called him, years ago, to give him news of her cancer, Clay remembered saying, "I don't know what to say," and she replied: "Just like when you were three." At her funeral, Clay couldn't speak. His older brother Raymond performed the eulogy. Why had the mutism returned? Perhaps language fled to its hiding spot, that original, pre-lingual dread of death.

As a toddler, Bradley exhibited similar problems with speech. His ability to use words was delayed, and when they came, they came out jumbled like a box of spilled matches. The boy could produce the correct words, but not the order in which to assemble them. His face would grow mottled with frustration, and he'd resort to pointing and screaming. Abbie was a speech therapist, so thankfully they had an expert in the house. In the afternoon Clay would listen to her with him, calmly going over their exercises. Clay knew he could never muster that level of patience with a child.

His childhood mutism engendered a deep-seated need, later in life, to find the right words. This was what drove him to want to be a writer. Eventually, this desire collapsed under the suspicion that there were no right words, that to be a writer was to nurse a wound with too-thin a bandage, and no anesthetic. The narrative he'd written about why his life with Abbie failed wasn't the full story. Before any of it—his retreat into alcohol and the dead world of television—something had already gone missing. To explain it was to string one word after another only to arrive at a paucity of meaning. The period at the end of a sentence was a bullet that killed sense dead in its tracks, and truth bled out the other end, lost to intelligibility.

WORK GREW slow during late summer. He watched more TV. He started drinking again. The Middle Eastern proprietors of the neighborhood liquor store became his surrogate family. He stalked the crumbling neighborhoods and dug through boxes of old books: Nausea, The Stranger, Journey to the End of the Night. Reading these again, they failed to generate the emotions they once did. It wasn't enough to be reminded how alienated he once was, and to enjoy this anger after the fact. He needed to get back to where words congealed to produce feeling, but could no longer locate that place.

DURING THE school's recesses, Clay took to sitting on his porch and watching the children play their senseless games. If he concentrated, he found he could absorb the entire pattern of their behavior. They moved with a terrifying compulsion: A ball kicked repeatedly against a concrete wall. A stick banged persistently against the rattling fence. A scream, a grunt, a scream. There was some terrible mechanism at work, one that had a purpose beyond the expenditure of energy. He felt there was a collective prayer they were attempting to communicate, a plea for salvation in a world spinning out of control.

ONE WEDNESDAY, Bradley was out front kicking the ball while Clay watched TV. He was on his third scotch of the afternoon. He heard Bradley talking to someone, and saw that he'd crossed the street, fingers clutching the school's fence. A small pug-faced boy with rusty hair stooped on the other side. He couldn't hear what they were saying. He focused back on the television, and when he turned to look again, Bradley and the boy were gone, replaced by a littered patch of grass. He got up to get a beer from the kitchen and, through the window above the sink, saw them in the backyard, huddled in shadows over a piece of paper.

"Who was that boy?" he asked later on, over pizza.
"I don't know," Bradley said.
"You didn't ask his name?"
"He doesn't talk."
"He can't talk? Or doesn't talk?" Clay asked.
"What's the difference?"
"There's a difference. Is there something wrong with him?"
"I don't know."
"What were you two looking at in the yard?"
"A thing he wrote," Bradley answered.
"What did it say?"
"It was in another language."
"Which language?"
"His own."

He attempted writing again. In his formative years, he'd work in the morning, before the critical faculties could mount their assault. But since the separation, the mornings had become too ugly to face. He'd loll in bed until ten, eleven, work until seven or eight. Then he'd eat something frozen and switch on the laptop. What came out was amateurish, incoherent. He resorted to getting drunk. On the fourth or fifth night of attempting to get something down on the page, a realization crashed over him with tidal force: the world was too wounded for writing.

He woke in the morning, head clanging, to find he had written this:

If the space between words is a suture, it is far too late for triage. A cosmic wound gushes torrents of ice-melt. Fires rain ash on all attempts to resuscitate the dead. I dream of Bradley, and his future. The dumb joy in his eyes, the obliviousness. His adulthood will be unlike any other in history. All the hurt caused by previous generations comes seething to the surface, ripening the contusion. Fresh bruises appear, in the news and on the planet's battered skin. Soon he will be old enough to realize, and there is no way for me to prevent it.

They saw more and more of the nameless boy. He and Bradley played their occult games, in the yard and in the attic. The boy would stay for dinner. They'd motion wordlessly to him, and he'd gesticulate in reply. He'd leave late at night, spilling his mute body into the dark. On one of their walks together, Bradley pointed out the boy's house—silent, roof canted, shingles chipped like broken teeth. Clay never saw the boy's parents; he came and went as he pleased.

In his games with Bradley, the boy often grew frustrated. He'd retreat to the closet and scrawl in a red spiral-bound notebook he carried with him everywhere. The closet became a favorite place for both boys—a musty alcove deep behind the shoe rack where they'd hatch their plans. Sometimes, the mute boy visited on days when Clay didn't have Bradley. Together, they'd sit silently and watch TV. Clay would look over at him and he'd be staring through the window. When Clay sat at his desk to write, the boy would open his notebook and fill the pages with his alien symbols deep into the night.

One evening, the boy left behind his notebook. Clay flipped through its mottled pages. At first, he thought it was a cipher and that there must be a key. He scoured the internet for information on code-breaking. He asked Bradley, and the boy reiterated that it was a private language, not a code. "How do you know," he asked, "if he doesn't talk?"

"He talks sometimes now," Bradley said.

"And he told you about this?" Clay said, motioning to a page in the notebook.

"Yeah. He said he has things to say that aren't sayable with words. Our words."

"What things?" Clay asked.

"If they're impossible to say, I can't tell you."

"When did he tell you this? I've never hear him say a word."

"In the closet."

"Has he taught you how to read this?" Clay asked, thrusting the book at Bradley's face.

"No one else can ever read it."

WHEN CLAY was honest with himself, he understood why he didn't talk when he was a kid. It was because he could sense things in his house, between his father and mother, that were too frightening for words. How his father would grow silent with rage at the dinner table over something inconsequential—a cold meal, a spilled drink. How his mother always went to bed earlier than anyone normally would. How Clay lived with the feeling that anything could happen and, when it did, there'd be nowhere to hide. He carried this affliction with him into adulthood. In all his years with Abbie, he never spoke his innermost feelings, how he loved her and depended on her. Why couldn't he say the simple, undiluted words *I love you*?

AFTER DROPPING Bradley at school, he scanned the pages of the boy's notebook into his computer. He converted the images into grayscale and heightened the contrast. He isolated each glyph from its neighbors and assembled them into an alphabet. Clay wasn't sure what the purpose was, but it felt like an attempt to get to the core of all that had been plaguing him.

Amid this work, Abbie called and accused him of "filling Bradley's head with nonsense." Apparently, Bradley had come home from his visit with Clay "white as a ghost," prattling about "a hole at the middle of everything." Clay said he didn't know what she was talking about. "Whatever it was you said, it scared him. I tried to get him to talk more about it, but he says that 'words signify nothing.' What is that supposed to mean, Clay? Please watch what you say. He's just a kid. He's very impressionable."

On his next visit, Clay interrogated Bradley. He refused to talk. When he pressed him further and threatened no dessert after dinner, Bradly pointed to the red spiral notebook. "You got it from this?" Clay asked.

"He told me what it's about," Bradley said, his face ruddy with shame.

"What is it about?" Clay demanded.

"You can't know," Bradley said, "you wouldn't understand."

"Don't tell me what I can't understand. Your mother seems to think I've filled your head with things and I need to know where they came from."

"It boy from the came me—he tell me—told—say not—uhh!"

Clay hadn't seen it in a while—the chaotic tumble of words, the frustration contorting his face. Clay wanted to embrace him, tell him he loved him, but words were futile. Instead, he turned away and switched on the TV.

Bradley was sullen for the rest of the visit. Neither of them spoke. The boy didn't come around. They watched TV together and Bradley went to bed early. Clay got drunk and sat down to write, but nothing came out.

He used a piece of open-source software to convert the boy's symbols into a font, loaded it into his system, and began to type. With the alcohol snaking through him, he felt the invented alphabet's power. He became a ventriloquist for a mythic god.

For the first time, he was writing with sheer conviction.

How freeing it was to write something no one could ever read.

That night, he had another dream. He was at his writing desk. The mute boy's hieroglyphics spilled across his screen. From them flowed an epiphany: It wasn't a paucity of meaning that infected language, but a surplus. It was all the things we were too ashamed to admit that prevented a chain of words from producing their intended purpose.

At his desk that evening, he became an artist for the first time. Writing words that no one could ever read was the birth of an unknown art form. For the first time, his work mattered, even if only to himself.

HE STOPPED. Through his door, he could hear Bradley weeping. He took in the empty bottles on his desk, the rubbish on his screen. He became alive to the senselessness of everything. The idiotic wobble of the trees' branches through the window. The chair in his office, inert, corpse-like. The houses lined up and down the street, arbitrary in their angles. The cars off on the highway, going nowhere, coming from nowhere. The breath in his lungs, a mechanical in-and-out that wasn't any more or less senseless than death.

Read these words: tree, chair, house, car, breath. Do these symbols, arranged arbitrarily on a page, mean anything? He had to abandon this language entirely. It was only what these things meant to him that mattered. And what they designated, they did so secretly, and the more private they stayed, the deeper their meaning became.

He woke with his head screaming and, with it, the sound of sirens. It felt like a sharp iron rod had been thrust into the back of his skull. He heard Bradley stirring in his room. His phone was ringing. He fell out of bed and crawled to the window and drew the blinds. Men with SWAT gear, clutching rifles, pushed across his yard. The stutter of automatic weapons fire came from the school. Shouts, screams, helicopters overhead.

He switched on the TV. A news anchor, stumbling over his words, was recounting a shooting. The footage cut to the ground, where a reporter was pressing a microphone to the mouth of a teenage girl. Senseless sounds spilled from her lips.

A classmate, a silent and strange redheaded boy, had opened fire on a classroom-full of students, and then himself.

There was a pounding at his door. Screams, shouts for him to open up. Clay looked at his computer's screen, bright and cruel in the shattered light, and the confession typed there, for everyone, and no one, to read.

A LOVELY FAMILY

i. Arrival

WE MOVED to the town after my wife accepted a position at the university. The house we purchased—a 1970s-era colonial covered in moldering wood shingles—lay just outside of campus, on the north side of town. Its yard butted up against a wooded area beyond which stretched the university's sports fields and recreational facilities. It was a mid-level school known mostly for its scientific research and football team. It brought a certain liveliness to the town, just enough to keep my interest, but not enough to make the town crowded.

At the time, I was going through a phase where I felt I wasn't in control of my own life. As it stood, I was the passive one in our relationship; my wife often took the reins, driving us toward whatever destiny she laid out for us. But this was beyond the ordinary. During the move, there lingered the sensation that I was being stripped of my identity, or, that it had long ago vanished and that the person I thought of as "me" was just a false veneer over old, dead wood.

The most striking symptom of this development was a partial amnesia or disembodiment. I'd lie awake at night, sifting through my past, the time before we came to the town, only to find sizable chunks missing, or blurred as if seen through frosted glass.

We arrived in the winter when students crowded the coffee houses and the streetlights favored the thoroughfares into and out of campus. The kids enjoyed running through the empty rooms of our new house, hearing their voices echo against the bare walls. There was a sleepiness to the town that I even felt when its roofs and gables were out of view. This, perhaps, was where my odd state of mind originated. The town drowned any thoughts that attempted to swim beyond its boundaries.

I telecommuted, so my job as a software engineer afforded me the ability to live half a world away from my clients. I set up my office in the house's attic. A small octagonal window looked out over the yard and the woods beyond. I spent an entire day connecting my computer's various cables, the printer, my speakers on which I listened to soft classical music while I coded applications and websites for a variety of corporate clients.

Eliza returned home at the end of each school day sleepy and with few complaints. The faculty was mostly friendly, the students engaged, if not overly bright. The university was once renowned for its pioneering work in cognitive science, but budget cuts had gutted the research department. A few researchers remained, Eliza being one of them.

On her fourth day of work, she came home talking about a rumor, one having to do with a faculty member who, in the '70s, had been engaged in controversial research involving student test subjects. It seemed quite a few participants in the study suffered from long-term psychological side effects. This scandal left a stain on the department which it never recovered from.

"What kind of research?" I asked over dinner.

"Something having to do with subjectivity and perception? There aren't a lot of details. He lived right here. In this house."

"You're serious."

"I'm serious."

"So was this a bad decision?"

"What?"

"The house. Taking the position?"

"No, don't be silly, Mike. It was a long time ago."

ii. Acclimation

Daphne, my oldest, started school with only a month left in the school year. Being a child dependent on rigid routines, this series of events—the move, the new school, the late start—sent her into a tailspin. She'd come home and throw herself down on her pink bedspread. I did my best to comfort her, although I felt that my world, too, was teetering at the edge of something large and undefinable, like a dark ocean.

Drew, our youngest, seemed to adapt just fine. He immediately made a friend named Barkley whom he played with at school and messaged with online. I never saw Barkley at school when dropping Drew off, but I heard much about him. I found it encouraging that Drew had so easily made a friend, something he'd struggled with in our old home town.

Soon after school began, however, Drew began experiencing health problems. He'd come home pale and tired, complaining of headaches. He lost his appetite and often left his dinner untouched. Eliza conferred with the school nurse, who promised to monitor it. I forced her to take him to a doctor who could find nothing the matter with him.

As for my relationship with Eliza, it was feeling strained. Often, when alone in the house together, I'd be seized by the sensation that I was an imposter. Occasionally Eliza would get a look in her eyes as if she didn't recognize me. And, stranger still, sometimes I felt I didn't recognize her.

iii. Spring Cleaning

Spring came, and the woods beyond my office window came to life. I watched the green spread like watercolor across a damp page. I spent a lengthy portion of each day procrastinating at the window, bathed in the changing light. The yard desperately needed cleaning.

I was engaged in a rather intense project coding a piece of investment-tracking software for a New York City-based financial firm, and I was starting to suffer tendonitis in my wrist.

"You're spending too much time at the keyboard," Eliza said. "You work from home. No one's keeping tabs. You should take breaks, go for a walk."

"The yard needs work. Maybe I'll get outside."

"Nothing strenuous. Call someone."

I heeded her advice, and made it my mission to leave my workstation at midday to take a hike through the woods with a packed lunch. In my free time, I'd hunt for someone to do the yard work.

On the first day, I found a secluded clearing about midway through the woods. From where I sat, I could hear the occasional coach's whistle from the university grounds. The sound had a narcotic quality, and I felt sleepy. I sat on a decaying tree stump, unpacked my sandwich, and found myself overcome by an unnameable anxiety. Birds chattered, trees leaned, my heart pounded. I am not one for soul-searching, but, after the fear passed, the occasion of its onset stuck with me. On the way back, I picked through my mind for causes of the episode and came up empty.

When I walked through the door, the phone was ringing. It was the school's principal, Mrs. Jackson; she told me that Daphne had been approached on the way to school by a strange man in a black Toyota. The man had told her he was a friend of her father's, and that he'd been sent by me to pick her up and take her to meet him in the woods behind the university. Daphne had stepped toward the car when—and this is the last thing she remembered—she heard a crackling sound like thunder and blacked out. The school medic said that it may have been a seizure.

"Seizure? What kind of seizure? A man in a Toyota? I don't know this man," I said. "Where is Daphne now?"

"She's here with us," Mrs. Jackson said. "She got through the first few periods before the episode—I believe—overwhelmed her."

"I don't know why she wouldn't say something right away, we've always told her—"

"Mr. Pope, the reason she didn't say anything right away was that she claims her mother was in the car with the man."

"Her mother? That's impossible. Her mother is at work and has been—"

"Mr. Pope, these things happen with children. Especially with those of Daphne's temperament. A new town, a new school. It's a lot for them to process."

iv. The Call

ON THE way to the school, I called Eliza and relayed the story. She seemed concerned but unalarmed. She laughed off the report that she was in the car with the strange man. "It must have been someone who looked like me," she said. She concurred that this was all perhaps too much for Daphne, who has never adapted well to change.

When I walked into the principal's office, Daphne was slumped across a chair with a lost look in her eyes. "Where's Mommy?" she asked when she saw me.

"She's at work."

"Who was that man she was with?"

"I don't think it was Mommy you saw. Are you sure it was her?"

She didn't answer, just looked at me through a film of tears.

On the way home, Daphne and I stopped for groceries at the local health food store. Outside the restrooms, on a bulletin board, I saw an ad for yard maintenance. The photo was of an elderly gentleman who identified himself as Jonathan. There was something strangely moving about the man's photo, even familiar. In it, he posed among trees, wearing overalls and holding a rake. His eyes were watery and bloodshot, as if he'd been crying. A surge of empathy came over me; he looked like he needed the work. No one had taken any of the small strips at the bottom of the sheet containing Jonathan's phone number. I tore one off and placed it in my pocket.

Daphne came out of the bathroom and gave me an odd look. "Let's go, Jonathan," I thought I heard her say.

"What did you say?"

"Why are you looking at me like that?" she said.

"Like what?" I asked.

"Like you don't know who I am."

v. The Friend

"Can I hang out with Barkley tonight?" Drew said to me the following Thursday night.

"It's a school night."

"It's just on the computer."

"Oh, you mean can you talk to Barkley tonight?"

"We hang out online."

"I suppose it's fine. Not too late, hear me?"

"Yes, Dad."

I'd learned early on that too-strict a policy regarding the children's social media usage would inevitably backfire. Whether we liked it or not, the kids were growing up in an unfamiliar world. When Eliza and I were young, the telephone was the social hub of the house. Friends called, we answered. We took to the streets and ran through yards. We measured time in bird chirps, the bloom of cicadas, sunsets and full moons. These days, it was likes and shares.

As a software engineer, I found it hypocritical to judge the new means of teen social life. We were all people, and we all grew up under the same stars. A secret conversation among school buddies was the same whether it occurred under a tree or via wireless signal. To treat this as an infraction of some philosophical set of standards was to cut the children off from what was becoming the only viable means of peer-to-peer contact.

Still, at night, alone, the unreality of the situation would nag at me. Was technology a viable means of human contact? Were words on a screen, illuminated by LEDs, edifying? Was what they gained—a feeling of belonging—enough to offset the warmth they lost in exchange? A new conservatism seemed to be rearing its head. Opinions I didn't accept as my own seemed to force themselves in on me from the outside. I was suddenly too old in my shoes, too sclerotic in my attitudes toward my children and the world at large.

vi. The Chamber

THE FOLLOWING Monday, I hiked to my favorite spot in the wood for lunch. It had rained the night before, and the ground was spongy and fragrant. Halfway across the clearing, as I made my way toward my favorite stump, my toe struck something in the ground. It did not feel like a root or a stone; it had the cold resonance of metal. I kicked at the spot with my shoe and heard a sonorous echo underground.

I got on my hands and knees and cleared a patch of loam from the area. What I revealed was a flat swatch of rusted metal, about a foot square. I felt around its edges and realized it continued in all directions. I stepped back to get a wider view; it looked as though someone had deliberately pushed leaves and soil over the object. Back on my haunches, I examined the ground and thought I could make out footsteps to and from the area.

I fished a sturdy branch from a nearby thicket and continued to scrape at the ground. The sun swam overhead, and all went silent. I looked at my watch and noticed nearly an hour had passed. My lunch remained uneaten, my stomach rumbled.

I cleared the rest of the leaves away and soon revealed a hatch—two rusty hinges, a seam caked with soil, and a latch. There was embossed lettering on the door, but it was hard to read in the glare. I wiped at the words with the hem of my shirt as sweat fell from my head and pooled in the crevasses. The words read:

DEPERSONALIZATION CHAMBER I

A WOODPECKER'S knocks echoed across the woods. I pulled at the hatch's handle and it swung open, revealing the first few rungs of an iron ladder descending into the gloom. A smell of mold and stagnant water swam up from the dark. I pulled my phone from my pocket and shone its light down inside, but the weak glow didn't penetrate far. The terror I'd felt on my first day in the clearing seeped back.

But something pulled me inside. I want to say it was curiosity, but it felt more like a return. Down I went into the musty shadows, plagued with the feeling that this was a homecoming of sorts. Eventually, my feet reached what felt like a tiled floor covered in an inch of water. Once again, I turn on my phone's light and examined my surroundings.

I was standing in a room, a cube approximately ten square feet in size. In one corner lay a rusty spartan cot covered in a wool blanket. An ancient mainframe computer with twin tape reels stood in the opposite corner. An old tube-driven terminal sat on a desk next to it. Behind me stood a set of sagging wooden shelves stocked with canned goods. From the labels, I could tell they were fifty years old, maybe more.

This was all strange enough, but what was stranger still was the sensation that I'd been here before. This déjà vu brought with it a surge of immense fatigue. It drew me to the small cot where, in the familiar silence, I spread myself out and closed my eyes.

vii. Jonathan

I FOUND myself back in the house, upstairs in front of the computer, with no recollection of having returned. As soon as I'd acclimated, the bell rang. When I opened the door, the old man from the yard cleaning ad was standing on the stoop, hands in the pockets of his worn overalls. In the driveway ticked the cooling engine of a black Toyota.

"Mr. Silver?"

"That's me."

"I'm Jonathan. You reached out regarding yard work?"

The scene in front of me—Jonathan in his overalls, the summer light drizzled across the lawn, the black car—had a fairytale quality. The impression that my wonderful life was an illusion seized me. I didn't recall having phoned Jonathan. Perhaps Eliza had, although I didn't remember mentioning him to her.

"Of course, come in."

Jonathan stepped into the foyer. There was something forlorn about his posture, as if his body were the locus of an immense loss. He scanned the framed photographs we had recently hung in a stair-step pattern next to the closet door.

"A lovely family," he said, moving from picture to picture. He lifted a hand to wipe something from his eye with one unsteady fingertip. I could have sworn it was a tear.

"Thank you," I said, wishing to move this along; his presence made me uncomfortable.

"My wife and I never had children," he said, still glued to the photos.

"I've got two you can have for cheap," I said. Just then he looked me in the eyes for the first time. I felt like I'd seen those eyes before, beyond the photocopied picture on the flyer at the market.

"Excuse me?"

"I'm being facetious."

"Ah," he said, not quite comprehending. My joke had opened a dull hole between us.

"Shall we look outside," I said, motioning toward the door. I wanted him out of my house as soon as possible.

"After you," he said.

We walked side-by-side around the house to the yard. The sun burst from behind a cloud and the temperature rose quickly. He rolled up his sleeves, and I noticed he had a tight bandage wrapped around his right wrist. He caught me looking at it and said, "tendonitis." I fingered my wrist, which throbbed. I made a note to swallow two ibuprofen once inside.

"You have a lovely family," Jonathan said again as we crossed the yard. "It was always my dream to have a beautiful family. I wasn't being entirely honest earlier." The sun fled behind the clouds, and the woods went dark. A breeze kicked up, and the trees danced. Jonathan glanced into the woods, toward where I'd found the underground room.

"Come again?" I asked.

"We had a child. Eliza and I. A little boy, Barkley."

"Did you say your wife's name was—"

"Eliza, yes. I know—what a coincidence."

"You've met my wife?" I asked.

"I came by the other day, you weren't here. She and I had a cup of tea."

"Oh, she didn't mention that. Barkley, did you say?"

"Huh?" Jonathan said. He had stared off into the woods.

"Your boy."

"Yes, yes. He passed."

"I'm so sorry."

"Leukemia. He put up a good fight."

For a moment, we stood among the sighs and moans of the yard. Then I said, "So, all these leaves and twigs should go. We'd like some new mulch put in around the beds."

"I've done work here before. It's all familiar to me."

"Oh, you have?"

"The prior owners used me."

"So, you have a general idea of what's required, then."

"I usually take my lunch in the woods, in the clearing. Is that okay with you?"

"Fine by me. I do it myself, it's nice."

"I can start tomorrow, does that work for you?"

"Sure does."

"You really do have a lovely family," he said as he walked away.

I WOKE on the cot in the dank dark. My rake lay propped against the wall. Above, the cold rim of daylight etched the shape of the chamber's hatch. It was time already to go; I wanted to stay forever. Soon the little girl would come sneaking through the woods, ready for her turn, and eventually, the boy.

I sat up and removed the electrodes from my head. For a moment I let the dream linger in my heart, where a tidal sob was just on the verge of breaking. Whoever had invented the room was on the verge of perfection. The dreams—if that's what they were—always began in a state of utmost joy, a crystalline believability. But then the distortions would set in, and slowly the facade would crumble.

I stood up and switched off the computer, and, rake in hand, climbed toward the hatch. Halfway toward it, suspended in the dark—much like I've been since Barkley died and Eliza left me—I paused and looked back down into the gloom. The machines, made by human hands, injected with a desperation for something better than we were given in the womb.

I opened the hatch and collected the trash from my lunch. As I'd done every day for four weeks, I carefully swept the soil and leaves over the hatch and took my old bones back through the woods. The wrist was acting up again. My lower back ached. My feet were sore.

In the yard, I continued my raking. Soon, fall would end and the winter would sweep in, and with it kill my ruse. I was too old for snow-clearing. In the window Mike was at his desk, staring into his machine's bright window, typing. Soon, the children would come home from school—a time I both dreaded and anticipated. And then, soon after, Eliza, who reminded me so much of my own.

I glanced up again at the man at his desk, and this time he caught me looking and waved. I wondered again if he knew how lucky he was.

WOW AND FLUTTER

THE SIGN advertising the estate sale is handwritten in black marker on day-glow green poster board. It is half obscured by tall grass, an afterthought. I turn off before I have a chance to think.

The house is set back among tired trees, a squat mid-century ranch with listless windows the color of aquarium glass. Across the street, a playground's swing drifts in the wind. A rusted seesaw leans like the wings of a downed plane.

There are no children.

October 31, 2022. Today is my birthday. My son and daughter haven't called. I'd spent the first half of the day at the mailbox, hoping for a card, but finding only junk. Ever since Eve passed, birthdays have been mere days on the calendar. I celebrate alone, over an expensive dinner at my favorite restaurant. I sit by the window, and watch families walk hand in hand down the boulevard. We think we are separate—souls wrapped in skin—but we are all one. We just need reminding now and then.

I am the only visitor on that slight afternoon. I tie the dog to a lamppost and walk inside. Most of the more valuable items have already been scavenged. An enormous homespun woman sits at a folding table in the garage's mildewed air with a cashbox and calculator. She smiles but remains glued to a paperback romance.

I drift through rooms lined with shag carpet and imitation wood panelling. It is a museum of tarnished brass and Bakelite.

I don't know how I know this, but a woman lived here, alone, carving out her final circumspect days. Through the picture window I see her in the yard. A radio plays oldies. She is wearing a floral print dress as she speaks with a faraway adult child on a cordless phone. She takes a sip of lemonade. An old dog runs in circles.

The scene vanishes—it is merely my fantasy of a life that was in all likelihood more lonesome, lived in desperate snatches. Deserts eaten from the pantry while standing in the dark. Quick trips to the bank to squirrel away savings. Birthdays spent alone, checking the mailbox for cards.

I stand in the low-ceilinged bedroom where she slept away fall afternoons much like this one. A closet with folding doors conceals a nest of wire hangers. Some of them are still cocooned in their thin paper sleeves printed with the logo of a dry-cleaner that no longer exists. A television's filmy black eye shows me myself. What am I looking for?

In the basement I find it—a box of cassette tapes. Their plastic cases are scuffed; their paper inserts yellowed. I rifle through them, fending off a sneeze. Some leaflets are blank; others are labeled in a small, neat hand: Christmas 1976, Jacob's Birthday 04/05/81, Phone Call With Melanie, Oct. 79.

"How much for the box?" I ask the woman at the table. She is eating potato salad from a Tupperware container. One of her plastic fork's tines is missing. She taps on her calculator as she chews and then says, "Dollar eighty."

"Your fork is broken," I say.

"I know," she says.

I fish two dollar bills from my pocket and say, "Keep it."

✳

I am a bank robber on a getaway. I drive home in the grips of the notion that within the box is something I've been seeking all my life. This expectation is tempered with the knowledge that if the tapes fail to reveal what I'm looking for, I will not have the strength to carry on.

My house feels unfamiliar. This tedious place is now the venue for a potentially life-changing discovery. I am hungry, but do not stop to eat. I descend to the basement and rummage through my old life. At the rear of one of the dilapidated wood shelves I find it. I climb the stairs with the machine trailing its cord like a black snake in the dark.

I pause halfway up, struck by the notion that the human race is coming toward the end of its history. As the song unspools, the mechanisms that give us hope are becoming worn, and will soon be obsolete. We will soon hear a heavy silence the world over.

I plug the cassette player in and sit at the dining room table, surrounded by walls of junk mail, catalogs, other detritus of life. I touch each tape to determine its potential. I must choose wisely; I don't have the heart to listen to all of them. All this week on the news: bombings, shootings, disease. The bloody face of a child makes its rounds through the digital sphere. I hope for deliverance.

✳

A magnetic tape's surface is a place of ghosts, hauntings. Ferrous oxide powder is arranged on a substrate of plastic film.

As the tape moves across the magnetic head, it displaces the particles into patterns. Upon playback, it translates changes in the field into a signal, and this signal is amplified. In the translation, there is loss: asperity, wow, flutter—the warble of the voices of the dead. The substrate is subject to deterioration. Slippage occurs, caused by hydrolysis of the binder to the tape. When overwritten, the powder's original patterns are seldom completely effaced; the spirit of each previous recording persists as an echo, a trace. In the hiss and crackle are stories, each laid over the next—the strata of lives, music, talk, memories.

I CHOOSE an unmarked tape. Something about its plastic skin suggests the embodiment of misplaced longing. The tape's spools turn like Mesmer's spirals. I hear the bias of gender—a woman's voice. The house listens:

"October 31st, 1981. My birthday. It was a cloudy day. The forecast was for rain. The children didn't call. Perhaps they've forgotten again. Ever since Aaron passed, birthdays are just another day. Every day is a birthday, if you want to stay positive. If sleep is like death, and waking a kind of birth, well then happy birthday to me! Not just today, but tomorrow and every beautiful day after.

"I tackle the day as I would any other. I clean, vacuum, take the dry cleaning into town. I put Tobey in the back of the car. He barks at the rain and whimpers when it thunders. It is just the two of us. We have fun together running in the park on the wet grass. Oh, if Aaron could see us now.

"It was an uneventful day. There's not much else to talk

about, except the record. On the way home the clouds were clearing. It was windy. The fall leaves went across the sky like hummingbirds. I felt like driving. Going home seemed lonely. I turned off into a neighborhood I didn't recognize. A small green sign was advertising an estate sale.

"When I pulled up there weren't any other cars. Perhaps the rain had scared everyone off, or perhaps all the good stuff had been taken. I tied Tobey up and went inside. I went from room to room. Mainly junk. All the stuff that people leave behind…in it they live on. But what does it mean to sell it to someone else? Perhaps this is how we form our connections, through objects. I felt relieved by this thought. Perhaps I wasn't a scavenger, but a Good Samaritan, helping the souls of the departed on their journey into the homes of others.

"Anyway, I didn't know what I was looking for. A birthday present for me, something to while away the day, a keepsake, a bit of connection.

"Then, I found it: an old box of records in the basement. Most of them were albums I recognized from when I was a girl, crooners and heartthrobs and long-haired men with guitars singing about one-night stands. All that silly sentimental stuff. Oh, the dreams we had back then…to be free, to be one body, united in love.

I PAUSED the tape. The room sighed around me. For the first time that day, my loneliness lifted. A great tension I'd been carrying within myself, like a taut wire stretched from heart to mind, relaxed. I wanted to dive into the tape's spools, flatten myself into a whisper, and revolve backwards in time to hold hands with this stranger. Through alchemical means they had reached out to me and plucked me from my painful individuality. I thought of the paltry amount I had paid for something so priceless. It is true: I was a thief. I pressed play—

"At the back of the box were several private-press records. Someone had gone through all the trouble to have their own albums made. My heart leapt: this was what I was looking for! Not something mass-produced, but personal, a touch of warmth on that rainy afternoon. The woman in the garage sold me the box for a dollar and helped me haul it to my car while Tobey barked at the sky. It started to pour again as I drove home. The records' mildew bloomed in the car's air. It reminded me of being a girl in my Nana's basement, alone with the spiders. Long summer days spent beside myself.

"Back home I knocked around in the basement looking for my old phonograph. I found it behind a box of mason jars. I scraped the fuzz from the needle and set the record spinning."

"'Hello Anna, hello Carl. It's your mother. I am recording this on October 31, 1954. It is my birthday. The war is over! There is so much hope in the air. The crowds have taken to the streets. I can hear them now. Listen: [sound of footsteps, a window sash being thrown up, cheers, whistles, horns]. I want to say that I miss you both. I wish you could be here with me to celebrate.

There is so much jubilance, but I've spent the day alone. But it's enough to know that a new day is being born, right here, outside my window. For now, I'll consider the future my companion. What a lovely companion it is. To all those people who may listen to this, maybe you've found me, in a secondhand shop or a yard sale or a cellar. I must sound like a ghost to you now. But I am alive and living. I'll stay with you like an echo down the years. Hear my message: there is hope.'"

Keith Rondinelli was born in New York in 1974. He is a graphic designer, illustrator, filmmaker, and musician. He lives in Ann Arbor, Michigan with his wife and two children. *A General Theory of Tears* is his first book.